DAUGHTER OF LIES

KENLEY DAVIDSON

PAGE NINE PRESS

Published by: Page Nine Press
Editing by: Janie Dullard at Lector's Books
Cover Design, Layout, & Formatting by: Page Nine Media

http://KenleyDavidson.com

For Jeff, who is everything a father should be to his daughters.

You have always been my Rom.

When the Queen heard the glass speak thus she trembled and shook with rage. "Snow White shall die," she cried, "even if it costs me my life."

Jacob and Wilhelm Grimm, *Little Snow-White*

～

PROLOGUE

The portrait lay on the desk, face down, with a pile of papers atop it, and yet she still wanted to look.

Someday, it would hang on the wall, where everyone could see. Someday, she would have a larger one made, so that everyone would know of her greatest achievement, but not yet. She could not afford for anyone to know just yet.

As she rose from her desk and moved towards the tea tray, she glanced impatiently at her reflection in the mirror on the far wall. It was so much like the portrait. She could not help tracing the curve of her own jaw, the straight line of her nose, and wonder at the similarities.

For so long, she'd been forced to pretend. To ignore her longing to hold and to love and to nurture the child she'd given birth to. Her husband had insisted that it was necessary. That their legacy could only survive if they were willing to accept the difficult

1

task of indifference, so that no one might ever guess there was anything amiss. But that requirement had eaten at her soul, day after day, year after year, and the gulf between her and her child had grown so vast that now all she had was the portrait to fuel her ambitions.

Those ambitions had grown over the years to a fire that burned deep and hot, a need that gnawed at her even as she sipped her tea, nibbled at a biscuit, and penned various messages. It waited, lurking at the edges of her consciousness as she gave instructions to her housekeeper, fielded questions from the butler, and planned her strategies for the upcoming weeks.

She was close—so very close—but winning was an exhausting business, especially when the entire kingdom wanted you to fail. Losing, however, was out of the question, so the woman accepted the possible consequences of victory, even as they nagged at her relentlessly.

Could she destroy her rivals without bringing about her own destruction? Would she gain what she most desired only to lose it again? And would the child she sacrificed so much for be willing to forgive her deception or would they be separated by the pain of all those necessary betrayals?

The eyes of the portrait seemed by turns forgiving and accusing, and on some days, she was almost afraid to look. But look she did, after setbacks and after triumphs, hoping to see the absolution she desired. Always, always, it eluded her.

She would not look today. She would wait, until she had taken another step closer to her goals. Well, perhaps until she had finished her messages. Or her tea.

Already she had begun to consider new alliances. Her plans were proceeding exactly as she intended—no, better—and only a few more pieces needed to be in play before her victory was assured.

Someday soon, there would be no need to gaze into the painted eyes of a portrait. She would look upon the real thing and beg for forgiveness. Beg her child to understand why she'd pretended for so long. On that day, she would come not as a broken supplicant, but as a woman who had survived the disdain of the world and was still unbowed, a woman who had gained power by her own efforts and could offer an alliance. She would have earned her victory over the forces that had always attempted to relegate her to the background of her own life, a forgotten pawn in the games so often played by men alone.

Before she was through, the Seagrave name would be rescued from the ash heap of history. No one would remember its failures, only its final success. She would prevail, and those who stood in her way would be vanquished.

On that day, she would have her child beside her, and there would be no more need for portraits.

But that day was not today, so perhaps a single glance… Smoothing her skirts, she locked the office door before retrieving the tiny gold-framed canvas from her desk and gazing anxiously into its guileless blue eyes.

The eyes in the portrait shone with all the promise of youth, alongside golden hair, an unlined face, and a charming smile. She, too, had been that young—that naive—once upon a time. She'd been dazzled by the promises of an older man, promises of wealth and consequence, promises of a place by his side. And she'd been fooled into thinking that he meant to share his power. But he'd meant only to smother her, moment by moment, into accepting his decrees and following his blundering course, and she'd had no choice but to pretend—to bank the fires of her ambition and shutter the passion in her soul.

For so many years, she'd pretended to be something she was not, and those years had not come without price. As she gazed at the youthful portrait, she pressed a trembling finger to the lines beside her eyes, across her forehead, at the corners of her mouth. They seemed longer, deeper, than they had been only yesterday. She knew it was impossible, but the thought frightened her. Perhaps she would try a new beauty treatment to hold them at bay, at least until after the wedding.

Though it wasn't as if her suitor would notice. He was strong, but gullible. Younger than she, but old enough to be desperate. He needed money. She needed a title. They were perfect for each other, and she expected his proposal any day now.

After they were married, he would discover she was nowhere

near so rich as he supposed, but by then, she would no longer need him.

First, however, there was a loose end to be tidied up. The woman shoved the portrait out of sight once more, and began to pen an invitation.

The end game had begun.

CHAPTER 1

My Dearest Breanne,

I realize that this letter may come as a surprise to you, given the manner of our only prior meeting. Until recently, any correspondence was forbidden by order of the earl, who felt that such a connection would be ill-advised and only serve to remind society of the unfortunate events of the past.

Allow me to assure you that I have always wished our circumstances to be otherwise. Had your father not insisted that it was for the best, I would have had the privilege of bringing up our heir as a beloved member of one of Andar's most ancient and respected noble families. Our firstborn child should never have been deprived of the opportunity to learn of the duties and responsibilities of a proud heritage, and I feel that this lack has been one of my greatest failures as a mother.

I very much regret the course of action to which your father persuaded me all those years ago, and beg you to believe that I wish very much to correct those errors which have led to the present state of our relationship. If you can find it in your heart to begin anew, I would feel privileged to have you as a guest in my new home near Camber. Crestwood is the name of the modest estate to which I have retired in order to remain out of the public eye, and though it may prove disappointing to one now accustomed to the grandeur of Norleigh, I hope that this will not affect your intentions regarding an extended visit.

It would be my pleasure to serve as your hostess for as long as your forbearance will permit you to stay. I have chosen to invite no one else during this time, as it is my fondest wish to spend the coming weeks correcting as many of my past failures as a mother as our time together will permit.

Please reply as to your plans, and whatever you decide, know that I remain,

Ever regretful,
Louise Seagrave

~

The force of the slamming door rattled the windows and made Countess Lizbet Norelle look up from her desk with an expression of mild curiosity.

"I quit," Brenna announced, pausing just inside the closed door to deliver her pronouncement as firmly and irrevocably as possible. "Resign. Abdicate. Surrender. Whatever it is that a countess does."

Lizbet placed her quill on her desk and leaned back in her chair. "A countess," she responded dryly, "smiles graciously at everyone no matter the provocation, while privately consigning them all to damnation. But she does not quit. And neither," Lizbet added, picking up her quill again with a slight smile, "do you. Which you will remember in a day or two and then be grateful that I have refused to accept your resignation. What is it this time?"

"My fourth proposal this week."

"So bad as that?" Lizbet's eyebrows twitched. "Any of them on their second try yet?"

"No." Brenna Seagrave dropped gracelessly into one of the rather uncomfortable chairs in front of her friend and former employer's desk. "All new. But with the same tired reasoning."

"No, don't tell me." Lizbet sighed and rested her chin on one ink-stained hand. "They all want nothing more in life than to remove the tremendous burden of responsibility from your delicate shoulders."

Brenna snorted. "My dear Lady Seagrave," she mimicked, batting her eyes beseechingly, "you must know how ardently attached to you I have become in the eternal three seconds we have known each other. Please permit me to express my undying affection for you and your money. Only marry me and I will be the happiest of men, once you relinquish complete control of your life and property into my hands, as you are clearly unfit to oversee them yourself."

Lizbet laughed, a soft sound of sympathy in the quiet room. "A clumsy lot, thank goodness. I'd hate to see you taken in by one who hid what he was and what he wanted until after the wedding."

"Small chance of that. I can't imagine putting up with any man long enough to marry him." Brenna shook her head slightly, as though she could cast off her frustration like a cloud of gnats. "You sent for me?"

Countess Norelle leaned over her desk and offered her former protégée a sealed packet. "The reports you requested have arrived."

Brenna took the papers and glanced at the front, where someone had scrawled her name in an impatient hand—"Lady Breanne Seagrave." The sight of it made her wince, and wonder anew what she could possibly have been thinking.

For years, she had been driven by bitterness over the knowledge of her parentage, wrongly believing herself to be the illegitimate daughter of Stockton Seagrave, Earl of Hennsley. In truth, she was his heir, but her parents had been unwilling to allow the estate to pass to a female. Instead, while she was still an infant, they had exchanged her for a convenient male child and allowed Brenna to grow up as a nameless orphan.

Fortunately, she'd been too driven to remain in a foundling home for long. Her skill with numbers and eye for detail had enabled her to establish a successful career as a member of

Countess Norelle's staff, at least until the previous year, when her family's deception had been discovered and made public. After a lengthy investigation and trial, the former earl and his heir had been stripped of lands and titles, all of which had been made over to Brenna, and she had become a celebrated member of court almost overnight.

She'd always wanted to be accepted. To have a family. She'd also wanted justice, but none of it had turned out quite the way she hoped. Except perhaps for Kyril, the second son of the Earl of Hennsley and therefore her younger brother. Brenna had resented the irritatingly charming young nobleman from a distance for years, and the beginning of their relationship had been far from cordial, but Kyril Seagrave had somehow become the best brother she could have imagined.

Otherwise, while it was satisfying to know that their father—the man most responsible for her lonely early life—would never profit from his actions, Brenna wasn't entirely certain that her life had changed for the better.

It had been a shock to realize that she liked being Brenna Haverly, clerk and occasional spy for Countess Norelle. The job had kept her busy, engaged her mind, and utilized her talents. She had been good at what she did, and she loved knowing that she was able to aid her kingdom.

But Breanne Louise Seagrave, Countess of Hennsley, seemed to be an entirely different person. She was a dress that didn't quite fit. Brenna (she refused to think of herself as Breanne) still didn't quite feel that she understood what a countess was supposed to do, but it was already clear that she was rarely, if ever, useful.

Unless that countess happened to be Lady Norelle. The pleasant, middle-aged, brown-haired woman across the desk was even more of an anomaly than Brenna had realized when they began working together all those years ago. But then, Lizbet was the king's sister-in-law and Prince Ramsey's aunt, so perhaps that explained how she had managed to establish both her authority and her ability so firmly that no one in the kingdom would dare to question it.

"Brenna, my dear"—Lizbet interrupted her thoughts rather abruptly—"I am very much afraid you are unhappy."

Brenna looked up from the papers in her lap, saw the expression on her mentor's face, and sighed.

"Why should I be unhappy?" she countered, not sure how to have this conversation with a woman who had once been her supervisor, and was now, in most ways, simply her social equal.

"Because you never asked for a life of privilege and you find it lonely, confining and utterly without merit in all other ways?"

Brenna made a sound that she intended to be a laugh, but it turned into something rather different as it emerged. It was not quite a sob. Not quite. "I'm sorry," she said, smoothing her skirts and looking fixedly at the floor. "I shouldn't complain. I *won't* complain. I have everything in the world to be happy about."

"Yes, of course," Lizbet said. "Everything except the things you most want. Like meaning, and purpose, and family."

Brenna's gaze darted up fleetingly. "But I do have a family, now. More so than I ever did before."

"You have a mother who has disappeared from society, a father who has chosen exile, a brother who pretends you aren't real and another brother who's been away in a foreign country for the last two months."

Lizbet's recitation was calm, but Brenna winced anyway.

"What would you have me do?" she answered caustically, preferring combat to showing weakness. "I tried being conciliatory, and look where that got me. And it isn't as though I would ask Kyril to give up his position in order to make my life easier. He is genuinely the best of brothers, but he has a complicated enough life without adding my concerns to his."

"I wasn't suggesting you try harder," Lizbet returned dryly. "Merely hoping you would stop denying the problem."

"Very well," Brenna replied. "I'm miserable. Is that what you wanted to hear? I hate being a countess. I preferred working alone in utter obscurity to dressing up and pretending that my title means something. I've tried managing the affairs of my estate, but no one at Norleigh seems to have any need of either my input or my oversight. The housekeeper acts like I'm an interloper and the bailiff treats me like a child so that I'm forced to argue with both of them constantly. I thought it might be less stressful staying here, but for the past month I've been desperately bored and ready to punch the next man who dares propose to me."

Lady Norelle chuckled. "Perhaps what you need is a change of scene."

"I would be happy to change my scene, but where would I go?"

Lizbet tapped her finger on her lips. "Well, I would suggest throwing a house party, but it sounds like returning to Norleigh is not quite what you had in mind." She grinned and waved her pen in the air. "It's also traditional to go visiting your friends' country estates when you're bored with court, but considering your antipathy towards nearly everyone, I'm not sure who I'd recommend that you visit."

Brenna snorted indelicately. "I certainly do not lack for invitations, but wherever I go I'm bound to be as overwhelmed by male attentions as I am here. I know quite well that the only point of those house parties is the formation of marital alliances."

"Unless you choose to visit someone who is unlikely to be interested in male company."

Brenna grimaced and thought back over her innumerable invitations. Most of them were from families with at least one or two offspring of marriageable age. There had been a few from desperate single males, who were probably only attempting house parties in order to lend an illusion of respectability to their pursuit of a specific woman. And then there had been that other invitation...

She'd ordered Faline to throw it away. At the time, she was quite certain she would never want anything to do with the sender. She'd been bitter, hurt and furious.

But now...

"I might have something," she announced thoughtfully. "I don't know that it's a good idea, but in the absence of a better one..."

"Is there any matrimonial intrigue involved?"

"None whatsoever," Brenna replied. "That I'm aware of. It was a personal invitation, from a woman."

"Is it far, far away from any of your ardent suitors?"

"I should think so." Brenna chuckled. "It's at least five days' journey to the northeast. Near the town of Camber."

Lizbet raised a brow in surprise. "I believe I have heard of Camber. Though I can't say I remember any families of note residing in that area."

"Not many. It's too wooded, but there are a handful of estates. Not wealthy ones, but enough to support the appearance of gentility."

"Sounds lovely," Lady Norelle admitted with a sigh. "There are days I'd rather enjoy running away into the woods myself, as Ramsey used to do."

"Used to?" Brenna echoed.

"Well, perhaps he does still disappear on occasion." She grimaced. "Though these days he's so nervous about Trystan's pregnancy that I can be assured he won't be gone long. So. Whose invitation are you considering accepting?"

"Louise Seagrave's."

Lizbet sat back in her chair and regarded Brenna with a studiously bland expression.

Brenna had been working for her long enough to guess at what it meant. "You don't approve?"

"It isn't so much that I approve or don't approve," Lizbet said. "It's more that I recall your vow never to have anything to do with the parents who cast you aside. Are you sure you want to give that woman a chance to wound you again?"

Brenna winced. "When you put it that way, I don't know that I'm certain, but I've been thinking about what I know of the situation, and I believe it's possible that it was never my... Louise's idea." She still had difficulty calling the woman mother. "Her letter seemed quite determinedly civil, and considering what a recluse she's been since I was named countess, I've wondered whether her refusal to see me could be out of embarrassment and shame, rather than rejection."

"Perhaps," Lizbet allowed. "And while I rejoice to see you feeling so hopeful, I would not be much of a friend if I permitted you to proceed without warning you that my experience of Louise suggests more than one possible interpretation."

Brenna slumped down in her chair. "And are any of those interpretations happy ones?"

"Difficult to say. Much of my impression of her is based on conjecture, I'm afraid. She was always quiet at court, while Stockton did all the talking. Though his style of conversation was perhaps better called blustering."

"That's what I'd heard." Brenna picked up one of the tassels on her dress and wrapped it around her fingers. "I thought it at least possible that Louise genuinely does want to know me, but is too shy of her reception at court to bring herself to visit me here."

"Yes," Lizbet agreed. "It is possible. But once again, I feel inclined to caution you. As I said, I know little of Louise Seagrave, and what I do know…" She broke off and stared at her desk. Lady Norelle appeared indecisive, which was not at all like her. "I don't know quite what to make of her, but I would encourage you to be on your guard if you do visit. I have never been able to determine her motives, and, as you are aware"—she grinned wryly at Brenna —"not knowing makes me nervous."

"Would you suggest that I reconsider the visit?" Brenna's heart sank a little. Part of her had felt a surge of excitement when she mentioned the idea aloud for the first time. If she decided to go, perhaps she could finally find out what had really happened all those years ago and lay the ghosts of her past to rest. But if Lizbet was worried…

"No," Lizbet replied decisively. "If you truly believe that your mother wishes to reconnect with you and you find yourself inclined to allow it, then I will wish you a pleasant journey and merely beg you to be cautious. As your friend. I have the utmost confidence in your judgement and your abilities, but I have no wish to see you hurt."

"Nor do I." Brenna stood and gripped her packet of papers a little tighter. "But if it's a choice between learning that Louise isn't really interested in me as a person and enduring another fifty marriage proposals, well… at least one of those I've already dealt with for most of my life. It can't really hurt me that much more than it already has."

"I hope you're right." Lady Norelle smiled, though the expression seemed a bit strained. "And I hope that I'm wrong. Perhaps this could be the first step towards escaping the past and finding something better for your future."

"Thank you," Brenna said, with a smile that was nearly as fake as Lizbet's. "I'll be sure to let you know whenever I decide."

Brenna was thoroughly engaged in muttering to herself when she pushed open the door to her rooms and encountered the very last person she would have expected to see there. And the second-to-last person she wished to see, ever.

"Eland." She pronounced the word with profound distaste.

Once the heir to the Seagrave properties, Eland was a tall, slender, cold-looking man with dark blond hair and a perpetually peevish expression. And that was before he'd been disinherited in her favor.

"Sister." He might as well have said "viper."

"Yes, well, that's a matter for debate, isn't it?" Brenna said nastily.

She probably should have been kinder—it wasn't as though Eland was responsible for the deception that had left her an orphan. He was as much the victim of her father's arrogance and lies as Brenna, and she'd hoped at first that they might find a way to be friends. She'd even dared to dream that he might be willing to embrace her as a sister, as Kyril had done the moment he first discovered their relationship. But Eland had been relentlessly unpleasant and condescending to her ever since they met, and Brenna was having a difficult time forgiving him.

"What are you doing in my rooms and do you need any special encouragement to leave?"

"I came only to see you, my lady countess, of course." Eland leaned back in his chair and crossed his legs. "Now that I am dependent on your generosity, I felt it only right that I should inquire how I might best serve you."

"I don't want your service," Brenna said bluntly. "I want you to leave my life alone. I will continue to support you because I'm not a monster and I know you have no skills beyond those you expected to need as an earl. But beyond that I'm not interested."

"That's not what you said when we first met," Eland reminded her smoothly, a slight whitening around his mouth betraying his agitation. "You were, at that time, rather more eager to make my acquaintance."

"When we first met, I was a naive young woman with no concept of the overwhelming self-righteousness practiced by most of the class that gave me birth. The last six months have done a great deal to rectify those... gaps in my education."

"And may I say," Eland returned blandly, "how very much

improved you are. A little polish has done wonders for your social presence."

"Out!" Brenna snarled, drawing herself up and pointing at the door, which might not have been very hospitable, but it was more hospitable than what she would have preferred to do. Stabbing him in the eye with a hairpin might have left a mark.

Eland rose and made a punctilious bow. "Of course, sister. I am at your command. And," he added, "as I wish only to prove my willingness to serve, allow me to offer a small piece of advice. A token, as it were, of my sincerity."

"Oh, do you have that?" Brenna asked snidely. "I was under the impression that our class avoided such things whenever possible."

"Well, we certainly attempt to suppress inappropriate outbursts of vulgarity," Eland said coolly. "But I'm sure you will find your way with time."

Brenna decided against further outrage. It would only make her insufferable "brother" happier. "Just say whatever you need to say and get out."

"I understand you have been suffering from an excess of proposals."

"That's hardly a state secret," Brenna muttered.

"I do not bring this to your attention as a way of improving my credit"—he seemed to hesitate—"but I fear it is not unheard of amongst my peers to resort to less than gentlemanly tactics in order to secure an advantageous marriage."

Brenna looked up at him, almost as though seeing him for the first time. Was he actually warning her that she might be importuned? "Are you suggesting that I might be compromised?" she asked baldly. "That someone might attempt to force my acceptance of a less than desirable suit?"

"Well..." Her ridiculous brother seemed slightly less pale. Possibly even a trifle pink. "Perhaps compromised is a strong word, but..."

Brenna burst out laughing. "My dear Eland, do you suppose the concept is foreign to my delicate ears? I once spent half a year keeping a tavern only a few streets from the docks. It isn't as though I don't know what compromised means."

"And that," Eland muttered, "is precisely why I warn you. There are fellows who might take your history as an invitation."

Brenna's insides turned to ice. "Fortunately, I am quite well-versed in the twisted reasoning common to the male gender in those respects," she said coldly. "I am also well able to defend myself from their advances. Perhaps you meant well, but it is not as though I required a reminder that I am commonly viewed as the future property of one man or another."

"But you will marry," Eland announced, quite without any doubt. "Or the earldom will die."

"No," Brenna reminded him, "it could very easily pass to a child of Kyril and Princess Ilani's. There is no particular need for me to produce an heir."

Eland's jaw dropped. "You would permit Norleigh to fall to a half-foreign brat?"

Brenna marched over to the door and yanked it open. "Go be an idiot somewhere else. Before I lose my temper and prove that I know how to deal with men who annoy me."

The former Seagrave heir was white to the lips as he stalked past her into the corridor, his fists clenched at his sides. "This conversation isn't over," he insisted. "You must reconsider."

"I am." Brenna smiled, showing most of her teeth in the process. "Currently I'm reconsidering allowing you to walk away with both of your eyes unblackened. If you ever insult my brother or his wife again in my hearing I will not be so forgiving."

Eland opened his mouth to reply and Brenna slammed the door in his face.

Perhaps she ought to thank him. If nothing else, he'd helped her come to a decision—she would accept the invitation to visit her mother at Crestwood. Considering the estate's distance from anywhere of interest, Brenna thought it reasonable to assume that she would be unlikely to see Eland or any other irritating men of her acquaintance for the duration of her stay.

At the moment, she couldn't imagine anything more sublime.

CHAPTER 2

*D*ear Sir,

  After a long search, your name has come to my attention as a man of many talents who may be equipped to assist me in a small matter of inheritance. I have been assured by multiple parties of your discretion, accuracy, and promptness in these transactions, and wish to discuss the potential for a contract that may be to our mutual benefit. In addition to the usual requirements, there is in this case some uncertainty as to the exact moment at which your services will be necessary. I am sure this comes as no surprise to one of your experience. If you are amenable, please reply to the bearer of this message as to your terms and availability, as well as any exclusions which may affect our contract.

\- *Grim Hill*

When Brenna's maid bustled into the room a short time later, she took one look at Brenna's face and put her hands on her hips.

"Eland?" she asked, wearing a pronounced scowl.

Brenna chuckled without much humor. "Was he making a nuisance of himself to you as well? Faline, you know you have my permission to evict him, forcibly if necessary."

"He insisted on waiting for you," Faline replied, "though I told him he and his nonsense weren't welcome. You know he's not much of one for listening. At least not to me."

"Not to anyone," Brenna assured her, taking a seat in her favorite chair and leaning her head back against the cushions. "At least not that I've noticed. But never fear—I sent him off with his knickers in a considerable twist."

The tall, straight-backed maid gave a nod of decided approval before kneeling down to remove Brenna's shoes. Or at least trying to.

"Faline, I believe I've told you I can take off my own shoes," Brenna reprimanded the dark-haired woman.

"Yes, my lady, you have," Faline responded meekly, standing up again with her hands folded and her head bowed. "But it is such a habit. You've no idea how hard it is to have nothing to do."

"Oh, don't I?" Brenna challenged.

Faline lifted an eyebrow and grinned at her mistress. "Perhaps, my lady."

Brenna snorted. She and Faline had been together less than a year, but it had taken only a few days for them to become more friends than mistress and servant. Their life stories were not so dissimilar—both had worked for a living from an early age—and, as Brenna had a difficult time permitting anyone else to do what she could very well do for herself, they had soon fallen into a familiar habit of bickering about most aspects of Brenna's life, from her need for a maid to current court fashions.

"And now that we're speaking of employment…" Brenna cast a glance at Faline from under her lashes. "How would you feel about going on a journey with me?"

The maid looked at her sharply, dark eyes narrowed. "I know very well you're not going to Norleigh, and you've told me a hundred times you'd rather die than go to any of these house parties. You've reconsidered, haven't you?"

Brenna sighed and reached down to remove her own shoes. "You know, sometimes I wish Lady Norelle had found me a slightly less perceptive maid."

"No, you don't." Faline took the shoes and carried them back into the bedroom before emerging again with a much-worn pair of slippers.

"All right, fine. I don't. You're right, that would be terribly dull."

Faline's cheek dimpled slightly in response to Brenna's admission, but she didn't respond, merely waited for Brenna to answer her original question.

"Yes," Brenna admitted finally. "I have reconsidered. Thanks in part to my horrible brother, I believe I may have finally decided to answer the invitation favorably. No matter what we find at Crestwood, it's unlikely to include Eland. Do you mind terribly?"

"What is it that you're hoping to accomplish, my lady?" Faline's expression remained neutral as she held out the slippers for Brenna to take.

Brenna scowled at Faline's outstretched hand. Or rather, she scowled at a question she didn't particularly care to answer.

She wasn't sure she knew what she hoped to accomplish. It seemed overly optimistic to believe that she might be able to forge a connection with the woman who gave birth to her. Was this merely an overly hasty decision that she would come to regret? An elaborate excuse to escape a life that was causing her to doubt herself more every day?

Brenna had once been a generally confident person—good at her job and entirely comfortable with herself. But somehow, becoming a countess seemed to have stripped much of that confidence away. These days she was uncomfortable with her position, her authority, even her clothes, and had a strong suspicion that she wasn't good at much of anything. And she had a strong aversion to mirrors.

As a spy, Brenna had never much minded what she looked like. Her lack of a classically beautiful face or a willowy figure had actually been an asset. It was far easier to pass unnoticed if one was not the style of woman most men considered attractive. She had found it a simple matter to be invisible and had often used her invisibility to her advantage. But now, she was expected to be seen. It was, apparently, part of her job as a countess to be stared at. Evaluated. Judged. And Brenna found herself wondering far more often— what, exactly, did everyone see? Did they see nothing but her title? Did they see her parents? Or did they see her? Breanne. Brenna. Worst of all, if they did see her, what did they think of what they saw?

Brenna hated the direction of her thoughts. Hated the perpetual feeling of discomfort with her own skin, the constant wondering whether there were things about herself that did not stand up to sustained scrutiny. Breanne Louise Seagrave attracted far too many assessing glances to ever pass in front of a mirror without wondering whether the short, frumpy blonde woman she saw in it was good enough.

The question that nagged her constantly was this: could she ever go back, or was Brenna Haverly, with all of her accomplishments and self-confidence, gone for good?

"I'm not sure what I'm hoping," she admitted to Faline. "I wouldn't say I'm running away, exactly, but I don't know that I hold out much hope for reconciling with my..." She glanced up wryly. "With Louise. Clearly I can't even decide what I ought to call her, so why should I expect our relationship to be simple?"

"Relationships never are, my lady," Faline said blandly. "Are you going for yourself, or because she asked you?"

Brenna shot her a withering glance. "Trust you to pose the

question I have been studiously avoiding. Because the answer is... I don't know.

She took the slippers from her maid and held them in her lap. "I suppose it's more for me. Not simply because I'm looking for an escape, but because... Well, because of *why* I'm escaping. I don't feel like I know who I am when I'm here. Am I Brenna? Am I Breanne? Do the court's expectations define me or am I still the same? Does it matter who my parents were?"

"You think that *woman*"—Faline did not hesitate to sound disdainful—"is going to help you find those answers?"

"Yes? No? I don't know, Faline." Brenna clutched her slippers tightly and tried to smooth the furrow in her brow. "I feel like perhaps I need to see her, to make my peace with what happened before I can decide who I am, or even understand the essential parts of being me. I feel like Brenna, but the world insists that I'm Breanne. Can they be the same person, or is the countess simply another role I'm playing?"

"Then I will be pleased to accompany you, my lady, no matter how I feel about our destination."

As she spoke, Faline continued to move unobtrusively about the room, shifting the lamps closer to where Brenna sat and fetching a basket with the day's correspondence. At first, there had been a tray, but it had proven unequal to the task of containing all of the notes and posies and tributes that her "admirers" had seen fit to bestow.

After sliding on her slippers, Brenna sorted through the

various messages, grumbling under her breath. "At least this embarrassing parade will be forced to direct itself elsewhere after we're gone."

"Don't be too sure, my lady," Faline warned her, a glint of humor in her eyes. "And wouldn't you say that persistence is a desirable quality in a man who hopes to win your heart?"

"If any of these"—Brenna glared at the basket—"have anything at all to do with my heart, I will be very much surprised. Now"— she looked up at Faline—"we should discuss packing."

Her maid nodded. Faline was much too well-trained to protest her mistress's plans, though Brenna suspected from her stiff posture and cool expression that she would have said a great deal more, if asked. Faline was fiercely protective, and never more so than when her mistress's status was called into question. The Seagrave family was a source of great irritation to her, though she would never be so improper as to say so unless such an impertinence was clearly invited.

"This should be quite a relaxing trip," Brenna remarked, hoping to allay her maid's misgivings. "It's a long journey, and it isn't as though there will be any other guests. We should be free to do as we please much of the time."

"Perhaps." Faline's eyes remained on her growing list of items that her mistress might require for her journey. "But not exactly comfortable. It's quite a remote area. If we forget anything, it won't be easy to come by, and if you find conversation a chore, there won't be a host of others lining up to share the burden."

"True," Brenna admitted, "but she invited me, after all. She must have some intention to put forth effort in order to establish a connection."

"One never knows," Faline muttered, a distinctly pessimistic tone to her words.

Brenna continued sorting idly through the correspondence in the basket, setting aside invitations to be responded to and discarding anything that seemed to be from a man likely to declare himself her devoted servant. At the bottom, however, she came across something far more interesting.

"Faline, why didn't you say there was a letter from Kyril?" she scolded, tearing at the seal with almost pathetic haste.

"Because then you wouldn't have even glanced at the rest and I would have been forced to nag at you for days to respond to your invitations."

Brenna grumbled under her breath about insubordination, but it wasn't serious and Faline knew it. The maid was smiling to herself as Brenna almost ripped the paper in her eagerness to read whatever her brother had seen fit to convey in his rambling, ridiculous style.

Dearest sister mine,

Would you believe it's even hotter here now than it was last time? Lani told me it would be, and the idea seemed so unlikely that I made the horrible mistake of smiling and saying "yes, dear," so she is now laughing at my misery and saying it serves me right. I suppose it does, at that.

Despite my constant complaining, we have been getting on splendidly and have had several very important meetings. Or at least, my beautiful wife has. Mostly I stand behind her chair and smile and generally look as stupid as I can. Don't even say it, sister. I know you're thinking something unflattering, and I'll have you know I can manage to look quite intelligent when I try.

Must say, I've been pleased to have the chance to acquaint myself further with Janard, though I'm not sure he'd say likewise. Very glad in either case that he's a friend. He's been a marvelous regent, and Zakir is turning into quite a commanding ruler, at least for a fourteen-year-old boy. At fourteen, I was living on pie and painting Father's carriage horses blue, which perhaps explains why Janard has turned down all of my requests to bring my brother-in-law back to Andar for a visit.

Two of Ilani's sisters have married, both to young emirs who seem less than completely stuck in the last century. They were among the first to make provisions for their freed slaves and have signed the provisional proclamation banning the harassment or persecution of mages. My dear wife scowled hideously at the poor fellows when she met them, but as Kanti and Tellara both seem happy enough, she did not quite resort to violence (though I suspect she threatened her new brothers-in-law with something dire when I wasn't looking, as they've been avoiding us ever since).

It would seem Varinda has been packed off to another part of the Empire, to practice her healing skills on the farmers and miners in a far eastern province. One hopes they sent at least a division or two of royal troops to keep her in line, as I would not care to be anywhere inside the borders of Caelan should she happen to escape. Which seems inevitable. Ilani says I'm being pessimistic, but as I am never pessimistic, that couldn't possibly be the case.

There is no word here of our favorite prince. He seems to have disappeared as thoroughly as you promised Janard he would, which seems a trifle suspicious, but then, he always does, so I will have to be content.

I hope you are well, sister mine, and that the court is treating you with courtesy, though I wouldn't wager any of my ambassador's stipend on it. If I had to guess, I would suppose that every unmarried member of the nobility from the ages of thirteen to ninety-three has tried at least once to propose marriage. And that you've refused them all and retreated to the family estate to brood in peace while harassing Wilkins unmercifully and re-calculating the books every day and a half.

My wife tells me I'm being insufferable, but I informed her I'm being my charming self and attempting to jolly you out of the sulks that you have no doubt fallen into during our absence.

Just promise you won't grow too grim. I'm sure, if you beg, Lady Norelle would be happy to engage your mind in one of her dastardly plans rather than have the newest member of Andar's peerage expire of boredom. Also, do keep an eye on Father and Eland. I don't wish to end this letter on a sour note, but they aren't what I'd call gracious losers, and may resort to making trouble. Though I rather suspect you would welcome it, if only for the excuse to punch both of them in the eye. Don't deny it, Brenna love, you know you would enjoy that immensely. As would I, which is why I beg you to refrain from doing so until I can be there to see it.

Oh, and could you expedite those reports I asked for? I would like to end our business here slightly ahead of schedule if at all possible, given the length of the return voyage and the fact that I want to spare Ilani any unnecessary strain or discomfort. She says she will be fine, but I'd rather not end up stuck here for another year, much as I enjoy my adventures with the local cuisine. Which is to say, not at all. I have finally discovered a total of three dishes that don't aggravate my stomach, and though my wife claims I am insulting the palace kitchens by insisting on them at every meal, I have at least not been spending the better part of every day visiting the necessary. Poor Ilani has been taking my place, so we will probably wait at least until that part of the business has ended before we attempt the homeward journey. Would never do to have both of us ill at once.

So we will expect to see you in two or three months, provided our business is concluded. Be well and be safe. You're no longer alone in the world, so be sure to take your poor dear brother's feelings into account before you risk your life on any more missions. I would so miss your stringent commentary on my life and wardrobe.

My wife says I'm being outrageous again, so now that I have accomplished my main goal in writing to you, I will end this letter with my fondest brotherly regards.

- Kyril

Oh, and Ilani has just now read the letter and whacked me over the head with a cushion for forgetting to mention that you're going to be an aunt. Cheers!

Brenna's mouth opened soundlessly and she lifted her head to stare at Faline, who was looking back with only mild curiosity.

"This…" Brenna started. She lifted the letter, then let it drop back into her lap. "This says…"

"Oh, are you going to be an aunt then?" Faline remarked, turning her attention back to the list in her hand.

"Faline! How could you possibly have known what it says?"

Her maid's expression may have been faintly superior. "I have sisters, my lady, and when they marry, it stands to reason that babies come along sooner or later. And I can't imagine you making that face for anything ordinary, like invasions or taxes or shipwrecks."

Brenna was surprised into a laugh by Faline's astute observation. It was true. Babies seemed far more terrifying at that precise moment. Especially one of Kyril's.

Could she imagine her brother being a father? Imagine him rearranging his life around a tiny person with his blue eyes and Ilani's face?

Yes, in fact, she could, and the thought made her both happy and deeply lonely. It was a good thing she was planning a trip. It would occupy her thoughts while she waited for this news to sink in. And it would ensure that she was gone from Evenleigh when Eland learned of it and came knocking at her door again.

Even if her visit to her mother proved to be a disappointment personally, Brenna could reassure herself with the reminder that the timing could not possibly have been better.

CHAPTER 3

*D*ear Sir,

  I accept your terms and am prepared to provide your usual requirements and fees. The name of your target is Breanne Seagrave, and I wish her eliminated at the most appropriate moment. It has come to my attention that she will be making an extended visit to a country estate near Camber in the coming days. Within no more than a week of arrival, she will be fleeing the protection of that estate, which should make your task a matter of utmost simplicity. There are any number of accidents that can befall an innocent young girl in the woods.

  Given your reputation, I foresee no need for further contact until your task is complete.

- Grim Hill

~

Brenna knew she'd made a mistake the moment she laid eyes on the towering wrought-iron gates of her destination. The house itself lay well back from the road, and through the bars she could catch a glimpse of the elegant line of its roof, of perfectly manicured gardens and of an elaborate marble fountain at the end of the carriage road. None of those would be particularly surprising or disturbing, had it not been for the gates, which swung open far too late for Brenna to miss the Hennsley crest at their center.

It was strange enough that Louise had managed to carve such beauty out of a rarely travelled corner of the kingdom. Not that the former countess hadn't the talent or the inclination, but where had she gotten the money? When the former earl had been stripped of his title, he had also been stripped of income, leaving his wife with little more than the inheritance she'd brought with her into marriage. No pittance, but neither was it more than a generous competence by the standards of the nobility.

And yet far stranger was her blatant use of the crest that no longer belonged to her.

Brenna was not particularly fond of her new title, but it was hers. She'd been cheated of it for far too long, and while she would not begrudge Louise her name, she couldn't help but feel uneasy about that crest. It was the symbol of authority. The sign of Brenna's birthright. An inescapable part of the responsibilities that came with her newly inherited title. What did it mean that Louise not only still used it, but flaunted it?

Brenna shared a glance with Faline, who didn't look nearly as surprised.

"Did you expect your mother to fall into poverty with a smile?" she inquired, her antipathy finally getting the better of her tongue. "Or to give up her privilege so tamely?"

"Her name is Louise," Brenna murmured. "And I don't know what I expected, but this wasn't it."

"You were hoping she had suffered a bit more for her betrayal perhaps."

Was that it? Perhaps it was, but if Brenna truly believed herself betrayed by the woman who gave birth to her, then why had she come? Why did she feel the need to form any sort of connection with a member of the family who had rejected her? She could barely stand to converse with Eland, and all she had against him was his own supercilious manner. Louise had been a far more willing party to the crimes of the past, so logic suggested Brenna should resent her far more deeply.

But logic and reason had little to do with the heart. Brenna could admit that part of her wanted to believe Louise had been forced into it. That if it weren't for the brutal, driven Earl of Hennsley, Brenna would have been raised as the pampered daughter of a noble house, rather than a nameless orphan.

"I suppose you could be right," Brenna admitted with a slight shrug. "No one ever accused me of being nice."

"At least, not more than once," Faline amended. "Are we going in?"

"We've come all this way. I suppose we'd better."

Neither of them spoke as the carriage made its way from the gates to the elegant double doors at the front of the house. The carriage path swept grandly around the cheerfully splashing fountain and forced visitors to disembark a full twelve steps below the entry, a deliberate design which permitted the owner to look down on guests from an immediate position of power.

More than ready to have the first awkward moments over with, Brenna tried to contain her impatience as they waited for the driver to open the carriage door for them—another "privilege" of her position. Another restriction that chafed.

The moment the door opened, Brenna nearly leapt out of her seat. Five days of travel hadn't helped her nerves or her temper, and neither she nor Faline enjoyed being confined in small spaces. No matter what reception awaited them, she would bear it with a smile for the sake of being out of the carriage.

No sooner had her feet hit the crushed gravel of the path than the grand doors of the house swung open to reveal a perfectly polished, uniformed butler, trailed by what seemed to be an army of equally polished footmen. They formed a precise line down one side of the steps, at which point Brenna expected to be greeted by their mistress, as courtesy required.

It was, however, the startlingly young and unusually attractive butler who stepped forward to bow, though the motion seemed perfunctory, and only just deep enough to avoid insult.

"Miss Seagrave, allow me to welcome you to Crestwood. Her ladyship is engaged with a guest at present, so she has instructed me to see to your comfort and then direct you to the drawing room after you've had opportunity to rest from your journey."

Brenna was still trying to digest the various stinging slaps delivered in those two politely phrased sentences when Faline stepped up beside her, dark curls springing free of their bun and brown eyes snapping.

"And who are you that you feel you have the right to insult a countess with your cheek?" she demanded baldly. "That's Lady Seagrave to you, no matter how you press your fancy uniforms or how fine you pretend to be. I won't be standing for any nonsense from the likes of you, not above stairs nor below."

The butler turned suddenly sharper blue eyes on Faline, and Brenna would have sworn he was fighting back a smirk.

"You are correct, of course, mistress," he said politely. "I do beg your pardon, Lady Seagrave. I am Danward, the butler here at Crestwood, and I must beg you to understand that I am only acting according to milady's wishes."

Faline sniffed. "Your lady has commanded you to greet her guests with insults?"

"As I said, I am performing the duties of my position, mistress," Danward replied stoically.

"And that'll be 'miss' to you, thank you," Faline retorted.

"Thank you, Danward." Brenna interrupted before the spat could develop further. "We would be delighted to have a chance to freshen up before appearing in company all rumpled from travel."

She foresaw a great deal of difficulty for her maid, being forced to deal with a household that had apparently not been instructed in the courtesy due a visiting countess and her staff. Not that Brenna minded for herself, but Faline was clearly ready to take it personally.

The golden-haired butler bowed again, a little more appropriately this time, and directed five of the footmen to assist with the ladies' luggage, while the sixth directed the driver to the stables.

Brenna and Faline followed Danward up the steps and into the house, and Brenna was once again reluctantly impressed with the opulence of Louise's new home. If impressed was quite the word.

Marble tiles, elaborately carved wooden panels, silk tapestries, brocade cushions... if the entryway was a reasonable example of the rest of the house, it might be even more lavish and excessive than Brenna's own.

Danward handed her over into the care of a maid whose face appeared to be as starched as her apron. After a brief, perfunctory curtsey, the maid led them upstairs to a bedroom which, to Brenna's eye, might never actually have been used. The furniture appeared new; the curtains, bedding, and upholstery were a perfectly matching shade of icy blue; and the rug was a vast expanse of unmarred white.

Brenna hated it. As soon as the door closed behind them, she sank down on the bed and was grateful to find that it, at least, was comfortable.

"If you remind me even once that you were against this from the start, I will send for Danward and have him set you to polishing silver," Brenna warned Faline, though her threat was as empty as her stomach after the long day's drive.

"Mayhap you should." Faline's expression grew calculating. "Might be I could discover whether all of this splendor is just a shiny bauble, to convince the world the former countess has not fallen so far as they think, or whether it's real all the way down to the bones."

Brenna snorted. "You can't fake that many footmen. And this house isn't exactly wattle and daub disguised as marble and granite."

"She could be in debt to her eyeballs," Faline countered. "Trying to keep this up in hopes of..."

"In hopes of what?" Brenna finished the thought. "Convincing her husband to reappear? Nobody knows where he is. In hopes of being accepted by the court? She's miles from everywhere and hasn't invited anyone else to see this place. I might not be aware of all the court gossip, but you can wager I'd be the first to know if she was sending out invitations again."

"Oh?" Faline asked archly. "Then who is it she's hosting in her drawing room? And why is it she's being so careful to keep them out of our way? You'd have thought she'd be eager to greet you, but there's no question she's not anxious for you to put in an appearance too soon."

Faline was right. Why wouldn't Louise bestir herself to greet them, unless she didn't want them to know anything about her guest?

Brenna grinned. "Suddenly, I'm feeling quite energetic. Now that we've arrived, I don't think I can wait a moment longer to greet our hostess. Surely she'll forgive my travel-worn state if I explain I was simply eager to see her again."

"I think she'll believe you've taken leave of your senses," Faline retorted, "but since I agree, I won't be the one to stop you."

Brenna didn't bother changing or washing or even allowing Faline to re-pin her hair. More than a little unnerved by her reception, she decided it wouldn't do at all to let Louise dictate the terms of their relationship. If she didn't want to rest, she wouldn't. If she decided to insist on being addressed properly, she would.

If. Brenna had yet to decide whether or not the servants' informal address bothered her enough to consider doing anything about it. She had never cared for her title for its own sake, so why should it irk her that Louise commanded her own servants to refer to her as "her ladyship"? The former countess had been stripped of everything—friends, home and position—and Brenna was now her social superior. What was so threatening about the fact that the woman was clinging to her illusions and living like a duchess?

Brenna hadn't made this journey with any real hope that her mother might somehow suddenly approve of her. Their first meeting the previous year had convinced Brenna that the former countess found her daughter lacking in every way that mattered. Louise had barely spoken, or even glanced Brenna's way—if anything she had studiously refused to acknowledge her oldest child.

No, Brenna had embarked on this trip with only the tiniest amount of hope that she might be able to connect in some small way with another member of her family. But if her mother truly desired to make a connection, why would she instruct her butler to greet her guests in a manner guaranteed to give offense?

As Brenna reached the bottom of the stairs, one of the interchangeable army of footmen appeared and bowed stiffly.

"Can I help you, miss?"

Apparently the order to omit Brenna's title also extended to the footmen, which meant she would be forced to make up her mind whether or not to object. If she insisted on being addressed as Lady Seagrave, she might appear to be insecure and jealous of her dignity. If she let it go, she might appear to be cowed by Louise's dictates and unwilling to challenge the former countess for her rights.

This was exactly the kind of game Brenna hated the most, and one of the reasons she had fled court. Apparently, she hadn't escaped her problems anywhere near so thoroughly as she'd hoped.

Brenna came to a decision, lifted her chin and gave the footman what she hoped was an imperious stare. "You certainly may," she said coolly. "You may address me as Lady Seagrave, and you may direct me to the drawing room at once."

The footman's mouth flopped open and then snapped closed. "I, er..." He floundered. "That is, my lady was not expecting you to join them... that is, her, just yet, miss... I mean, my lady..."

Brenna took pity on him. It wasn't his fault his mistress was delusional.

"The drawing room," she repeated. "At once."

His face went pale, but he bowed and turned on a perfectly polished heel, leading her swiftly to a pair of wide, carven doors at the rear of the house. Brenna could hear voices from within, slightly raised. One delicately female, the other deep and decidedly masculine. Was Louise entertaining gentlemen?

The idea struck Brenna with some force, but there was no time to consider it. The footman pushed open the doors and preceded her into a bright, sunlit room, bowing towards the left wall as he announced, "Lady Breanne Seagrave, my lady."

Brenna entered behind him and immediately turned her gaze to the small blonde woman holding court on a settee in the corner. The settee was positioned carefully to afford a commanding view of the room, but it was the woman's expression that Brenna noticed first.

She was decidedly annoyed.

Louise Seagrave was not quite fifty, but appeared much younger. Her eyes and mouth had begun to show lines, especially when pinched with disapproval, but she was still a regally beautiful woman. She was dressed in the height of fashion, her golden hair was elaborately bound with silvery-blue ribbons, and the hands resting in her lap were smooth and perfectly manicured.

At their first meeting, Louise had seemed quiet and self-effacing, deferring in everything to her larger, louder husband. At present, however, the tilt of her head and the challenge in her eye caused Brenna to wonder whether that could have all been an act.

"Breanne!" Louise smiled, but it was not an expression that made Brenna feel particularly welcome. The older woman also remained seated, which further punctuated her insistence on granting herself precedence in her own home. "I thought you were going to rest, after such a long and tiring journey!"

"I thank you for the offer, but I'm not the least bit tired," Brenna said politely.

"Well, I'm sure I instructed Danward to inform you that I had another guest and would greet you as soon as I was able," Louise said, "but perhaps he was remiss."

As much as Brenna had not cared for Danward, she couldn't allow him to be reprimanded for her decisions. Nor did she care to let Louise believe that she would be easy to manipulate.

"Oh, he mentioned it," she said brightly, advancing further into the room. "I simply couldn't wait to begin renewing our acquaintance."

"Hmmm." Louise smoothed her dress and patted her hair with one delicate, be-ringed hand. "I suppose there's little harm done. And I am so glad you've finally arrived, Breanne, dear. I had expected you several weeks ago, but perhaps my invitation was not delivered promptly."

As if Brenna could not possibly have spent those weeks contemplating refusal.

"I am delighted to be here," she responded mechanically, eying the available chairs and wondering whether she ought to simply sit down, despite the absence of an offer. "But I'm afraid I must insist that you call me Brenna. After twenty-eight years, I simply can't seem to accustom myself to Breanne."

Hah. Louise's icy smile became a grimace carved from marble.

"Of course, Brenna. I will be sure to instruct my staff and visitors accordingly. I wouldn't wish to make you feel uncomfortable in any way."

Brenna nodded, a single, genteel bob of the head to show that there were no ill feelings.

"And now, I suppose I ought to make introductions," Louise continued, turning to her right, where her prior visitor stood with his back turned, seemingly staring into the fire. "Rommel, my friend, permit me to introduce my daughter, Miss Brenna Seagrave."

The man turned, and Brenna had to force herself not to take a step back when she realized how enormously tall he was.

"Brenna, this is Lord Griffin, my nearest neighbor and a newly arrived resident of Camber. He has only recently purchased the estate to the west of Crestwood and hopes to make it his home."

Fighting back a sigh, Brenna made her curtsey, aware that by Louise's design, she now appeared to have the lowest rank in the room. More properly, the introductions ought to have been reversed. What did Louise hope to accomplish with this snubbing? What did it mean that she had clearly not intended her guests to meet? And if this man was her friend, ought Brenna be wary of him as well?

His initial appearance suggested wariness would be wise. He was positively the tallest, broadest man Brenna had ever seen, though none of that size was due to excess. But the longer she watched him the more she wondered whether he was anywhere near so imposing as his height would suggest. His bow was slow and deliberate, and though his features were generally handsome, his expression appeared lazy, touched with only mild interest. His gray eyes met hers with congeniality, but without so much as a smidge of curiosity. Though that could be due to their respective ages—the gray in his somewhat rumpled brown hair indicated he was at least some years older than Brenna herself, though not so advanced in age as Louise. Probably about forty.

"Miss Seagrave," he said slowly, in a voice that rumbled like an earthquake. "I am very much afraid that I'm intruding on a joyous family reunion."

"Nothing of the sort," Brenna replied brightly. "Louise was kind enough to invite me and as I had nowhere else to be, I decided a short jaunt to the country might prove refreshing."

She heard a quick intake of breath from Louise.

"But... Breanne."

Brenna glanced over to see a look of hurt steal over the woman's face.

"I most explicitly said in my letter that I hoped to reconnect with you. It is my deepest desire to make something better out of this disaster your father..." She paused and collected herself. "...that the earl has made of our family."

It was possible that she meant it. That all of her delicate snubs were nothing more than a carefully constructed delusion, meant to keep despair at bay. But Brenna wasn't ready to forgive and forget quite so easily.

"Perhaps there will also be opportunities to explore our familial connection," Brenna agreed affably.

"I, for one, intend to find this a cause for celebration," Louise insisted. "My daughter has been restored to me and it is a source of both consolation and joy."

Not surprisingly, her face indicated neither emotion.

"My lady, I have just had the most marvelous idea," Lord Griffin announced in a ponderous, plodding tone. "I simply must have you both to Lorenhall." He favored both ladies with a smile, but slowly, as though it dawned across his face like the rising sun. "We shall have a picnic, to celebrate your reunion."

"Oh, but, Rom," Louise protested, "I couldn't possibly put you out by expecting you to entertain us both. We will be spending our time getting to know one another, and I'm sure our conversation would prove to be of little interest to a bachelor. I believe it would be best if we put off our little visits until after Brenna has returned to Evenleigh."

She smiled up at him in an unmistakably flirtatious way, forcing Brenna to suppress a gag. What was the woman thinking, batting her eyes at a man ten years her junior?

Lord Griffin, however, hadn't seemed to notice. Or if he had, his response was as delayed as his smile. "Nonsense." He waved off her protests. "We are neighbors, and all that. I'll expect you around the end of the week. Send someone round with a note, and I'll be sure to have the gardeners prepare the west lawn."

"Oh, but..."

"I won't hear of any objections," he insisted, in that deep, rumbling voice. "And now I'll take myself off. I fear I should be very much in the way now that your lovely daughter is here to keep you company."

"No, of course not!" Louise mustered an excessive degree of polite enthusiasm for this rebuttal. "And thank you, my friend, for your kind invitation. I'll send someone over with a message about the best day for our picnic. Does that suit you, Brenna?"

"Oh, decidedly." It wasn't as though she'd been left the option of disagreeing. "I would be most delighted to pay a visit to your estate, Lord Griffin." Brenna would mostly be delighted because Louise didn't appear to want to go. It was quite clear that Brenna hadn't been intended to make Lord Griffin's acquaintance at all, and now she thought she knew why.

Was Louise really making eyes at a man with the intention of trapping him into marriage? True, Stockton Seagrave had been missing for a little over a year. Under Andari law, that made her a widow, entitled to inherit his estate and free to marry again. But was she really so desperate as to go after the first man she could find? Lord Griffin was a peer, true, but he was quite a bit younger, and not exactly sharp-witted.

Or could it be that the two of them had been a couple longer than anyone might suspect? That Lord Griffin had been part of Louise's decision to move to Camber in the first place?

A single hour in her mother's house and Brenna was already regretting her decision to come. She ought to have gone to one of the numerous house parties that had begged for her attendance. At least there she would have known what to expect. Here, she could very well be trapped in Louise's bizarre retreat from reality, where titles were dependent on Louise's own inclination and the past could be ignored if she chose.

~

After enduring three endless days of her mother's company, Brenna was more than ready to assert that a picnic was exactly what she wished for. Even if it required her to watch Louise flirt with their lumbering giant of a neighbor.

Brenna had joined the former countess for meals and for tea, for embroidery in the drawing room, and for one painfully awkward walk through the gardens. Thus far there had been no mention whatsoever of the past, only a bewildering recitation of the merits of Crestwood, a litany of the many offenses against her, and innumerable paltry attacks on Brenna.

They were so small and so gently phrased that at first Brenna barely noticed, but after a time she could hardly avoid being stung by them.

Over breakfast, there had been comments about her wardrobe.

"Brenna dear, that dress is just a trifle low cut for morning, isn't it?" Followed by a self-deprecating laugh. "Oh, I am sorry, I suppose you haven't had anyone to guide you in the development of your taste. Never fear, my dear"—a motherly hand on the arm —"I shall be sure to remedy that while we are together."

While chatting over tea, there were animadversions on her conversation. "Breanne—oh, I am sorry—Brenna, I don't mean to make you uneasy, but perhaps you did not know that it is considered somewhat unseemly for ladies to speak with quite so much volume, especially when indoors."

During their attempt at embroidery, Brenna's lack of ability with a needle was remarked upon, just sharply enough to annoy even Brenna, who cared little about such domestic skills.

"Child, I know your upbringing was not what it ought to have been, but did no one teach you the importance of a neat and tiny stitch?"

At luncheon, her style of eating came in for its share of censure.

"I feel certain that I should tell you—that bite was just a trifle larger than what might be considered acceptable in the best company."

And on their outing in the gardens, even Brenna's gait was criticized.

"Your stride, my dear. Perhaps you might moderate it, especially when in company with gentlemen."

On that occasion, the helpful commentary was followed by a lowering of lashes over Louise's enormous blue eyes. "I understand that I should have been there to help you all along…" She broke off with a tiny hiccup that was probably supposed to be a sob. "And I know that my attempts now may be unwelcome. But I wish to assure you, with all my heart, that I do not say these things to shame you. Only to help you, in the event that you ever decide you wish to marry. We cannot, perhaps, overcome all of your disadvantages,"—she shot Brenna a look of sorrow and sympathy—"but I feel certain there would be several men of appropriate fortune who could overlook deficits of style in favor of the attractiveness of wealth."

Brenna did not even have to feign her indigestion, and retreated to her room to have a headache and castigate herself for dreaming of reconciliation.

She'd had sufficient etiquette lessons as part of her training to feel assured that her decorum was beyond reproach and her manners unexceptionable. Those criticisms she could easily dismiss as jealousy, or even an older generation's stricter standards. The comments regarding her person, however, were more difficult to brush aside, perhaps because they hit a little too near her own insecurities about her appearance.

But truly, it mattered little whether Brenna believed in the truth of the observations or not. Clearly her "mother" hoped to make her daughter over in her own image, or perhaps to revive her self-consequence by pointing out that the current countess was nowhere near so beautiful and accomplished as herself.

Louise gave every indication of being fully as weak, self-centered and dependent on the perception of others as Brenna had long assumed, and as Lizbet's vague warnings had no doubt been intended to convey. Brenna should have listened to her mentor's instincts, and her own, which had always insisted that a woman who could so easily surrender her own child for the sake of power could never truly be a mother in any but the most basic sense of the term. For some reason, Brenna simply hadn't been willing to give up.

After this, however, she should have more than enough evidence to convince her to admit her mistake and move on. There was nothing to grieve, because there had never been anything there in the first place, except Brenna's foolish, scarcely realized hopes.

"Faline," she remarked, as she readied herself for bed on the third night, "whyever did I promise by letter that I would stay for at least two weeks? I don't think I'll be able to bear this for even two more days."

Her maid looked over from where she was rearranging dresses in the wardrobe. "Are you perhaps forgetting, my lady, that you are under no obligation to this woman? She may have borne you, but then she gave you away without a backwards look. A few days of self-pity can't change the past, and you don't owe her more than you've already given."

"No," Brenna admitted, "but we still haven't discussed the past, so I can't truly judge her for what happened all those years ago. Maybe it wasn't her idea. But even if that turned out to be true, I find that it's the present I'm struggling to forgive her for now." She picked at a corner of the bedspread, feeling irrationally pleased when the seam parted beneath her fingers. "She can't seem to find anything about me to approve of, and she's spreading her judgements throughout the household. Even her servants feel like they have leave to correct me! Her personal maid actually shushed me yesterday morning!"

Faline snorted. "Aye, it's ridiculous and you shouldn't be forced to put up with such impertinence, but believe me when I say it was never their idea. They've been given specific instructions on how to go on."

"Really?" Brenna sat up, her eyes narrowed. "Faline, you've been holding out. Tell me what you've learned downstairs."

Her maid came over to sit on the bed. "Are you sure you want to hear it? It seems to me you still harbor hopes of your mother's redemption. I shouldn't wish to interfere, if you truly intend to find out the truth of the past."

"I don't know that I care anymore." She did care. She just didn't want to, and anything Faline had to say would only help douse those ridiculous embers of hope.

"Then I can tell you that her orders all come through that Danward fellow. I don't know how he was ever hired, as he's hardly older than the footmen, but he runs an orderly household and knows everything about everyone."

"And you're sure it's Louise, and not Danward's idea for them to be insulting?"

Faline shook her head. "For all that he's young, and a bit too sharp to my way of thinking, he's not one to set his own rules. Besides, I've heard him talking of it, when he didn't know I was close enough to hear. He said the mistress had given instructions that everyone was to watch you and either report or point out your mistakes."

"And he doesn't suspect that you're watching him?" Brenna felt a sudden jolt of unease on behalf of her maid—no, her friend.

"Faline, you're alone here, but for me, and you could find yourself in danger if they suspect that you've been spying on them."

"And what are they going to do to me?" Faline asked, one dark eyebrow arched. "I can take care of myself, my lady, and I've made it my business to be friendly and obliging. Except to that Danward fellow—he's too smart by half and I don't trust his looks. Also, he sneaks out at night, at least once a week, or so one of the chambermaids tells me. He could be engaged in something more than half shady."

Brenna laughed. "I think you're simply unused to attractive butlers. You can bet that every maid for miles around has noticed his youth and good looks, same as you—he's probably just sneaking out to meet a sweetheart."

Faline scowled. "You may joke of it, but it's a fact that men like him don't often hold such a position."

"Hopefully he doesn't find out that you think him young and attractive," Brenna remarked slyly.

"And how is it that we're talking of me, now?" Faline folded her arms and glared at Brenna. "What we should be talking of is what you're going to do about all this. If you're unhappy, why not just leave? We could be going home tomorrow."

"I don't know, Faline." Brenna flopped back on the bed. "All she's done is subject me to humiliating personal remarks. If I cut and run now, she'll know she's hurt me, and that may mean she's won whatever insidious game she thinks she's playing."

Faline offered an evil smile. "Well, if you're not interested in running, my lady, there are other options. After all, weren't we agreed that no one has ever accused you of being nice?"

Brenna pursed her lips and folded her arms. "Perhaps you should tell me what you have in mind," she said, beginning to smile rather evilly herself. "Because at the moment, you are correct. I am feeling anything but nice."

CHAPTER 4

*L*ord Rommel Griffin cursed his employer under his breath as he tied his cravat for the fourth time that morning.

The first time he hadn't been paying attention and the knot had been far too neat. The second looked like a child of four had tied a bow around his neck, and by the third attempt, the cloth had been too wrinkled and had to be discarded.

His hair was too long and it itched. Neither his boots nor his coat fit, nor did this life he was pretending to enjoy—and they wouldn't for as long as it took to complete his mission. And now, because he had not yet managed to obtain the evidence his employer sought, he was about to be forced to play host to a pair of catty females who—his man on the inside informed him—had lasted barely a day in the same house before drawing up the lines of battle over issues so ridiculous as the length of one's sleeves.

Rom could have been halfway across the ocean by now, sailing into a new port as advisor to one of His Majesty's ambassadors. But thanks to the ridiculous knee injury he'd sustained when jumping off a roof near the Trentham docks in pursuit of a smuggler, he'd been put on enforced rest and assigned to surveillance.

Rom wished he'd hit that smuggler harder once he'd caught him.

He'd heard of Breanne Seagrave once or twice since his return from a two-year mission to Vidor. She was rumored to be an overnight heiress and an amusing novelty at court, though he hadn't stopped in Evenleigh long enough to have met her or heard much of the gossip. It was only because of his present task that he knew as much as he did.

Dispossessed first daughter of the Earl of Hennsley, Breanne had taken over the earldom when her father's deception was discovered. Her early life, by all accounts, had not been easy, and could have done little to prepare her for her new role, though she'd presumably found an education somewhere. Even a brief meeting had been sufficient to ascertain that she was far more genteel than one would expect given her upbringing. Perhaps she had not attended to all the proprieties, but then, neither had Louise.

Of course, his opinion of Breanne had been formed at least in part by what he'd heard of her from her mother, though Rom considered every word out of Louise Seagrave's mouth to be highly suspect. According to Louise, the girl was sadly neglected, poor dear, and a bit of a disappointment in both looks and deportment. Louise had extensive plans to groom her into something resembling respectability so as to eventually find her a man who could overlook her less desirable qualities.

But that was coming from a woman who couldn't seem to admit—even to herself—that she'd lost both her title and her position, and had instructed her servants to snub the new countess at every available opportunity.

During the few minutes he had spent with the newest Lady Seagrave, Rom had seen nothing out of the ordinary. She had a pleasant face, an attractive smile, and a very keen pair of blue eyes, though her manner had been bland enough.

What he couldn't be sure of was her motives. Why had she come to visit the mother who had so comprehensively rejected her? And why had his employer asked him to keep an eye on her while she was there?

It added another layer of complexity to his task, and Rom didn't like it. He wanted to get this over with and get back to real work. But until his man could acquire the evidence they both needed, he was stuck. Stuck pretending to be the sort of fellow who had no objection to squiring a pair of simpering women about his purposefully neglected grounds until they were bored enough to leave again. Stuck enduring the none-too-subtle hints of a woman over ten years his senior that she considered him a suitable prospect for a second marriage, now that her first could officially be dissolved.

The rattling of carriage wheels indicated that his time for whining and regrets was over. His visitors had arrived and he would need to become the man he pretended to be in company—slow and genial, a countrified member of the gentry with no pretensions to fashion or intelligence. A man Louise Seagrave believed she could easily manipulate.

Next time he decided it would be a brilliant idea to leap off a roof, he was going to have his head examined.

By the time his guests descended from their carriage, Rom was already waiting to receive them, his lips stretched in a pleasant expression of welcome. The elder Seagrave was the first to appear, and she had clearly exerted herself to please. Her dress was new, in a flattering style, and her hair had been arranged so as to conceal her age as artfully as possible.

Breanne, by contrast, appeared in the doorway of the carriage wearing a dress designed for an evening out, in a cut entirely unsuited to her generous curves. Her shoes were almost-nonexistent sandals and her blonde hair gave the impression of having been styled in the midst of a windstorm.

But she was smiling as if nothing was amiss, and accepted the hand of his footman with an outpouring of elaborate thanks.

Rom could be mistaken, but this did not seem like quite the same woman he'd encountered in the drawing room at Crestwood only three days before.

"Lady Seagrave, so happy you could come. Lady Seagrave." He

bowed, hoping he'd managed to offend at least one of them. "It's an honor to host two such beautiful ladies. I confess that I now feel quite ashamed at the state of my grounds. They're well enough for a bachelor, but not quite the thing for welcoming guests."

"Rom, you mustn't make yourself uneasy on my account," Louise said demurely, casting her eyes down and offering him her gloved hand. "We are far too close of friends by now to judge one another by our estates."

Which was why she'd been going out of her way to make him believe her a wealthy widow ever since he moved in next door.

"Of course we are," he agreed, kissing her hand before turning to her daughter.

"Miss Breanne, so honored you were able to join us."

She giggled. For some reason, it didn't suit her at all.

"Oh, but the honor is all mine, sir," she demurred, mimicking her mother's downward glance, but without any effective pretense of shyness. "Louise has been explaining how kind it is of everyone to be patient with my missteps in society, and how I ought to make every effort to be grateful to those who condescend to receive me despite my unfortunate coarseness of manner." She leaned forward and winked. Actually winked. "Too many years on the docks, I suppose."

It was all Rom could do to maintain his placid, bovine expression. Definitely not the same woman. Louise had frozen in evident horror and appeared to be searching for words to cover the embarrassing revelation.

"But," Breanne went on, "Louise has promised that she will be well able to teach me how to present myself with the style befitting a countess, considering that she used to be one, you know." This was uttered with blithe unconcern for the effect it was having on its subject, who appeared to be choking. "I must say, the lessons have been quite instructive." Breanne leaned closer as if to impart something in the nature of a secret. "I had no idea it wasn't quite the thing to discuss one's stockings in public, or to mention how many fellows I've kissed, or to brag of how many sweet rolls I can eat in one sitting."

"I suppose not," Rom agreed solemnly, but only with a great deal of effort. He wasn't sure he'd ever had to work so hard to hold back laughter. "Much more appropriate conversations for young gentlemen, I believe."

"But not for true gentlemen, of course," Louise stated, casting him an imploring glance.

"But of course, Lady Seagrave. I do apologize." Whenever he was with Louise, Rom made a habit of agreeing with everything. It made him sound like a fool and relieved him from the burden of deciding what sort of opinions he ought to hold given his present facade.

"Now then," his elder guest said brightly, looking desperate to change the subject, "what do you have planned for us today?"

"Well now, I thought I might show you both around the house and the grounds, and then my cook is preparing a picnic, provided the weather stays fine."

Considering that it was sunny and warm without a cloud in sight, this was, of course, a rather silly thing to say, but Louise clutched at his arm and glanced at the sky in alarm.

Breanne burst out laughing. It wasn't a genteel sort of laugh, but more the kind that rang out above everything in the vicinity—a genuine expression of amusement.

"Louise, I do believe you are flirting with poor Lord Griffin." She fluttered her eyelashes. "At least, you're going about it exactly as I would if I wished to attract a handsome fellow. Fancy thinking that it might actually rain on a day like this." She let out another peal of laughter while Louise's face turned an alarming shade of red.

"My dear," she said between gritted teeth, "did we not discuss that it would be more appropriate for you to call me Mother? And of course I am not flirting. Lord Griffin is my friend and neighbor, that is all."

"Is that how you explain it so as not to seem forward?" Breanne's eyes widened innocently. "Thank you, Louise. I'll be sure to use that strategy next time I meet a man and wish him to know I'm interested."

"Mother," Louise insisted.

"Oh, but I couldn't." Breanne paused to adjust her neckline and fiddle with her numerous bracelets, before looking up with a bright smile. "It simply wouldn't feel right. There's something about the word "mother" that doesn't seem to fit you at all."

She shrugged, and that's when Rom began to wonder whether Lady Breanne Seagrave was quite the person she appeared to be.

It didn't take long for her to confuse him even further. What had become of the Lady Seagrave he had met at Crestwood? She hadn't said much, but she had seemed reasonably educated and polite. This Lady Seagrave was going out of her way to be as unpolished and uncouth as possible, and yet managed to accept every one of her mother's reprimands with cheerful equanimity.

When he led the ladies through the overgrown gardens at the back of the house, Breanne clapped her hands and exclaimed with delight.

"It's just like a wilderness, don't you think, Lord Griffin? I'm delighted with how the forest seems to be growing right in the middle of your lawn."

When he showed them the drawing room, where he almost never set foot, she exclaimed in horror at the state of the furniture. "I declare, a room like this makes me want to give it a good dusting," she said, her hands on her hips. "Perhaps I could borrow some rags and polish? I could have it looking good as new in no time."

"A lady does not dust," Louise said, her tone a bit hollow by now with fatigue.

"Then should I fetch a servant and command them to dust?"

Breanne inquired. "I feel as though I have a great deal of under-standing of what a lady does *not* do, but no one has yet bothered to be clear about what it is a lady *does* do. Certainly nothing amusing."

"But ladies do so many things." Rom felt moved to contribute to the absurdity of the conversation. "They dance and draw and paint and sing and read improving books."

"Yes, but as I already said, nothing amusing," Breanne retorted. "Gentlemen may ride about doing as they please, shooting and hunting and looking out for agreeably indolent ladies who will go on doing nothing once they're married. And if some poor girl happens to be unable to paint or sing, what's left?"

"I suppose she might read some more."

"Indeed, she might," Louise interjected in a glacial tone, "but she does not ever, ever argue with gentlemen."

"Oh, but we were not arguing," Breanne insisted cheerfully. "We were discussing. Or is that another activity that is not encour-aged for ladies? I realize it's not quite the thing for gentlemen to find out that we have ankles, but should they also not be permitted to discover that we have thoughts?"

Rom choked, and barely managed to disguise laughter as a fit of coughing.

"I believe it may be time for our picnic," he said hastily, as soon as his coughs had subsided sufficiently to allow for speech. "Please do be seated, ladies, and I will inquire of the cook whether our basket is prepared."

Even with the door closed behind him, he could hear Louise's voice as she began castigating her guest for various misdeeds, both real and imagined.

Rom couldn't help but feel a bit sorry for the new countess. She'd discovered a family, only to find that she hadn't any hope of pleasing them or fitting into their lives. It was probably fortunate that she was so obliviously cheerful, or Louise's diatribes might have wounded. Though perhaps they did, even if she didn't show it.

No matter what class you were born to, a mother ought to be a person who comforted. A father should be someone you could rely on. Breanne had neither—no one who was willing to teach her what she needed to know with patience and understanding—and Rom could empathize with the lack.

His own parents had died when he was only ten, leaving him and his small estate to the guardianship of an uncle, who had loved and cared for Rom as if he were his own son. But his uncle had also died young. Rom had been left alone in the world, and would probably have fallen prey to the many temptations available to young noblemen had he not been taken under the wing of Caspar Norelle. The older man had encouraged him to keep his wits sharp and seek active employment, which he'd done. Rom had spent the past fourteen years serving the Crown all over the world, with the result that he was rarely ever in one place for long and preferred it that way. In fact, he'd sold his estate a few years back and never once regretted it.

He did, however, occasionally wish that he had someone to

come home to, whether that home was a townhouse, a farmhouse, or a set of rented rooms in Evenleigh. If he ever was fortunate enough to have a family, he would certainly never abandon or betray them, as it seemed Stockton Seagrave had done many times over.

But it was highly unlikely that Rom would ever have such a thing. He was home too rarely, and his lifestyle would never be called settled. He could not imagine asking a wife to wait for him, even if he happened to find one that would be willing.

After his distressingly short walk to the kitchens, his cook informed him that the picnic was already set out on the west lawn, so Rom reluctantly made his way back to the drawing room where Breanne was now thumping away discordantly on his ancient, out-of-tune clavier. Louise was sitting stiffly erect in her chair, making no attempt to hide her disgust.

"A creditable performance," he announced, as soon as there was a pause in the cacophony. "But I believe our picnic has been prepared, if you would care to join me?"

Breanne jumped up from her seat. "Delighted, Lord Griffin," she proclaimed brightly. "All this playing has made me hungry as a bear." She paused, then giggled and shook her tangled blonde curls. "I suppose I ought not have said that. But I am hungry, and I don't see why stomachs are another thing young ladies must pretend they don't have."

Rom didn't disagree, but it wasn't like he could say so in front of Louise. He settled for a vacuous smile and offered both ladies an arm, reminding himself firmly that he only needed to keep them occupied long enough for his man to search the study at Crestwood. He also needed to ensure that he didn't give Louise any encouragement in her pursuit.

He had leased the rundown estate merely to provide proximity to his target, and had been almost instantly taken aback by the change in his neighbor's behavior. Between her deliberate displays of the luxuries of her home, her flirtatious conversation, and her blatant attempts to make herself appear younger, the former Lady Seagrave had done everything she could to signal that she was wealthy and available, a potentially desirable match for an aging peer in need of a rich wife.

Shocked and somewhat appalled, Rom had found it increasingly difficult to disentangle himself from her advances, while still remaining friendly enough to gain access to her life. Perhaps in that respect Breanne's visit could actually be of benefit. He could pretend to be taken with her, and thereby convince her mother that she would need to look elsewhere for a titled husband. Rom was willing to do a great deal for king and country, but he wasn't about to be trapped into marriage by a calculating harpy.

So, as soon as they reached the west lawn, he devoted himself to Breanne, and listened to every word of her nonsense with the appearance of enjoyment.

Louise grew visibly more and more agitated, until at length, when they had finished eating, she rose to her feet and smiled at Rom. "I have spied a lovely little gazebo at the far end of your lawn, Lord Griffin. Would you be so kind as to escort me while I stroll over to take a closer look?"

"I am at your service," he said, rising slowly to his feet and brushing off his ill-fitting coat. "Lady Seagrave, would you care to join us?"

Louise's lips pinched together as Breanne smiled sunnily and shook her head.

"I wouldn't dream of interrupting your time together," she said, with a sly wink at Louise. "And Lord Griffin, since it seems we may someday be related, I give you leave to call me Brenna."

"But is your name not Breanne?"

"I suppose that was the one I was born with." She shrugged. "But no one who has cared for me has ever called me that, so I should much prefer that you call me by the name I have chosen for myself."

Rom winced at the implication. "Of course, my lady. And as we are to be neighbors, I must insist that you call me Rom, as your mother does."

"Rom, you cannot be serious," Louise hissed, as soon as they were out of earshot. "To be making up to her in that ridiculous way? It's going to turn her silly little head and she's too inexperienced to know that you're only having fun at her expense."

"She might be a trifle innocent, perhaps," he replied cautiously, "but she's quite pretty, you know. And she doesn't seem to mind that I'm not as fashionable as some men. I don't think she would pout if I came in to dinner in my riding boots, and it isn't like I could support a wife who insisted on all the latest styles."

He glanced over and observed the blood draining from his companion's face.

"Rom. Are you actually..." She clutched at her skirts. "You're not thinking of making my appalling daughter an offer. I thought I was clear about her need for guidance, her social inexperience... everything! She's hopelessly gauche! And you've only known her a few days!"

"Well now, as to that..." He stammered a bit before coming to the point. "I don't know. But there aren't that many ladies here who are interested in a lord with more land than money, especially one who, as my dear mother used to say, has more meat than merit, and is past his best years." He laughed ponderously at his own lame attempt at humor.

"And of course it has nothing to do with the fact that she's a countess," Louise interjected bitterly.

"Well, one does have to think of these things after all," Rom said apologetically. "An estate doesn't run itself, you know. And there's not much income to be had here in the midst of the forest."

"I see." Louise lifted her chin and dropped his arm. "I believe I've changed my mind about the gazebo. The sun has grown too hot and I have developed a sudden headache. Please be so kind as to call for my carriage at once."

"My dear Louise, have I offended you in some way?" Rom babbled his way through an apology, but his guest was obdurate, and he ended by scurrying off to the stables in relief to inform her driver that the Ladies Seagrave were ready to depart.

Perhaps he had overdone it a trifle, but he doubted Brenna Seagrave would be sharp enough to detect his feigned interest. Even if she had, she was convinced her mother desired to attach him, and there was simply no way Louise would inform Brenna that the object of her pursuit preferred her daughter.

No, he should be safe. And if his man at Crestwood had managed to obtain the proof they sought, his sojourn in the inhospitable wilds of Camber would hopefully come to a close before too many more days had passed.

CHAPTER 5

Dear Sir,

I find that circumstances beyond my control necessitate a hastening of your task. Some improvisation may be necessary, but please recall my advice as to the preferred method and proceed at the earliest possible moment. Despite the unexpected urgency, I continue to expect swift, silent, and untraceable action. Send word by the usual messenger when your work is complete.

- Grim Hill

Brenna could not remember ever being so exhausted. Faline's evil plot had been even more effective than she'd anticipated, but it took work to pretend to be quite that stupid. It had been worth it though—Louise had been satisfyingly appalled. She wanted an unpolished, unacceptable daughter? Then that was what she would get. And if Brenna's antics embarrassed her mother in front of the object of her romantic pursuit? So much the better.

Lord Griffin, unfortunately, had proven much harder to discomfit. The man was so relentlessly agreeable, trying to fence with him verbally was like sparring with a feather pillow. The hits simply sank in without him noticing. His every move was so slow and deliberate, Brenna was sure she could see him thinking it through before he took a step or lifted a bite of food to his mouth.

There at the last, she had almost begun to wonder whether he was showing signs of romantic interest. At least, he'd appeared to hang on her words, and laughed at things that Brenna intended to be more shocking than funny. It was a novel experience to attract a man's notice for her wit rather than her money—even a man so slow of thought as Rom—but no matter. She was sure that after her performance, Louise would redouble her efforts to prevent any further meetings between Brenna and the shambling, shaggy-haired Lord Griffin.

In fact, Louise didn't seem all that enthusiastic about spending time with Brenna either. She'd been resolutely silent and stone faced on their return to Crestwood, and disappeared into her study shortly thereafter. Brenna dined alone after Louise pleaded a headache, and returned to her room afterwards to confer with Faline and decide what she was going to do next.

"I can't stay here for the whole two weeks," she informed her maid decisively. "It will drive me mad. As amusing as it is to toy with Louise, it's also disheartening and I don't believe I can keep it up."

"Perhaps not," Faline agreed. "But mayhap you ought to think about staying for at least a short while longer." Her expression grew calculating.

"Considering that you appear to have interesting news, I'm willing to entertain the idea," Brenna replied, sitting on her bed and leaning back onto a mountain of pillows. "What have you learned?"

"Not so much what I've learned as what I've observed." Faline sat primly at the foot of the bed and cast a disparaging glance at Brenna's posture.

"After the day I've had, you'd lounge about as well," she muttered, sitting up with an enormous sigh. "Happy now?"

"I'm only looking out for your welfare," Faline insisted with a tiny sniff.

"Oh, stuff it." Brenna rolled her eyes. "And tell me what you've *observed.*"

"I observed that insufferable butler, Danward, rifling through his lady's desk," Faline announced coolly.

Brenna sat up a lot straighter.

"Insufferable, how? And did he find anything?"

"Insufferable with his perfect hair and his perfect teeth and his perfect manners that never slip so much as an inch, even in the servants hall," Faline complained. "He's so perfectly polite I can't tell a thing about him but I could swear he's laughing at me."

Brenna chuckled. "I think you like him."

"I do not like him," Faline snapped. "And I don't know if he found anything. I watched him go through several drawers, including a secret one behind a bookshelf, and he seemed to know exactly what he was looking for."

"Well, that is interesting, I must say," Brenna mused. "If it were anyone else, I would report him for such behavior. However, I can't say that Louise doesn't bear watching, considering my own questions about how she's obtained the money to keep this place up. Do you think him the sort who would attempt theft?"

"I doubt it," Faline replied. "He was looking more closely at papers, reading over them before moving on to the next. It was information he was after if you ask me."

"Lizbet did warn me to be careful." Brenna wondered if this could have anything to do with her friend's vague suggestions of caution. Was Louise involved in anything shady or illegal? It could be that she'd obtained her money by somewhat questionable means. Or it could be that her inheritance had been larger than anyone knew.

"Perhaps we will stay an extra day or two," she announced, drawing a laugh from Faline.

"Never could resist an investigation, could you?"

"That's terribly unfair," Brenna protested. "I've barely investigated anything since we've known each other."

"Oh, and that explains why you are always sending off for reports and shuttling packets back and forth from Lady Norelle's office."

"I have not the smallest idea what you're talking about," Brenna said loftily. "And now I think it is time for bed before I incriminate myself any further."

She dressed for bed, lay down and blew out her candle, but Brenna had no luck whatsoever falling asleep. She kept wondering whether this trip had been a mistake, whether she ought to just ask Louise what had truly occurred when she was born, or whether she should simply return home and allow it to be a mystery.

The answer wouldn't change what had happened. And, as things stood, it wasn't likely to change her relationship with Louise. The woman was critical, self-centered and cruel.

But she'd also been under the thumb of a critical, controlling man for much of her life. Was that not some excuse for her behavior? Could she change, given the opportunity?

Brenna's eyes were just beginning to drift shut when she became aware of a slight breeze that she had not noted before. One of her curtains twitched slightly, and the barest whisper of a footstep caught her ear.

Had she been any other countess, she probably would have either screamed for help, dismissed the disturbance as a night breeze, or lain frozen under her covers while waiting for her fate. Brenna reached for the knife under her pillow and prepared for an attack.

Another suggestion of sound emerged from the dark, and before Brenna could move, there was a man standing by her bed. His silhouette loomed over her in the moonlight, one hand holding a naked blade. It wasn't pointed at her, but she wasn't about to wait for him to decide where to strike. She threw her blankets at him, leapt out of bed in the opposite direction and set her back to the door.

The man made no move to follow her. "Mrs. Delaney," he said, in a flat, emotionless voice. His tone was low and uninflected, offering not the smallest hint of what sort of person might have spoken. "You've made a valiant effort, but you know you can't escape."

Whoever he was, lover or assassin, he'd gotten the wrong room. Brenna started to tell him so, until memory caught up with her. She had once *been* Mrs. Delaney, but only on a secret voyage to another country that had nearly ended in disaster. No one had reason to know that name, except maybe...

"*Quinn?*"

"You were expecting some other assassin?"

Brenna choked on her retort. "Pardon me if I wasn't expecting any assassins at all. What are you doing here?"

Silence met her query.

"Quinn, why are you in Camber and what are you doing in my room?"

His answer held neither interest nor emotion. "I was hired to murder you."

It was such a Quinn thing to say. No opinions, just the facts. Except when the facts were that someone wanted you dead badly enough to pay for it, it would be nice if the message were conveyed with some sort of sympathy.

"I see." Brenna lowered her knife. "Nice to see you too. Haven't heard from you in a while. How have you been? Please pardon me while I consider my last requests."

"You shouldn't lower that knife," Quinn replied coolly. "I've been paid to cut out your heart."

"Yes," Brenna said with a sigh. "I'm sure you were. Boohoo, woe is me, and all that. Now put up the sword while I stoke the fire. It seems you have some explaining to do."

Quinn did nothing so normal as sheathing his sword, sitting down, or even leaning against the wall. He remained armed and alert while Brenna found her wrap, stirred the fire, and added coal. When it was burning well, she lit the room's lamps and sat on the edge of her bed to regard the gray-clad intruder with a quizzical eye.

"Since you announced yourself rather than simply relieving me of my life, I must assume you meant to warn me. We both know you could have killed me in my sleep. Who hired you?"

"If I knew, I wouldn't have bothered warning you." Quinn's remarks were always cryptic, but this was a new low.

"So if you knew who hired you to kill me, you would have just killed me?"

"I would have relieved them of their delusions that I'm a killer for hire," Quinn corrected. "My services are often used as bait. I was paid by a proxy—a man who does odd jobs here in Camber—and Lady Norelle wants to know who's behind it."

"When were you hired? And where?" That might limit the possibilities.

"Thirty-four days ago, in Evenleigh."

"Why, Quinn." Brenna pressed a hand to her heart. "You were in town and didn't even stop by to say hello to an old friend? I'm crushed."

Quinn didn't so much as smile, because Quinn never smiled. The nondescript sandy-haired man was possibly the most stoic Brenna had ever encountered. Ever since their adventures in Caelan, she had gone out of her way to provoke him on every meeting, hoping to at least draw a smile or some tiny indication that he thought of her as an acquaintance. Assassins, he had once insisted, did not have friends.

But no matter how he thought of her, Quinn had been an integral part of their success—and survival—in Caelan, and no group could go through such trials together without forming a bond of some sort. Irritating as he was, Brenna was glad to see him.

"So, you were hired by an unknown person to rid the world of my presence, and tracked me all the way here hoping to do what, exactly?"

"I was hired to stay close," he said. "Wait for the right moment. Whoever wants you dead, didn't want it to happen right away, and they didn't want it happening in Evenleigh."

Brenna wrinkled her nose as she thought that through. "I suppose that means the appropriate moment you were waiting for occurred this evening."

Quinn jerked his head in a quick negative. "Received a new message. Said I should proceed as quickly as possible."

"And do you have any particular suspects?" Brenna found that she rather dreaded his response.

The assassin said nothing for a moment, while his expression remained as inscrutable as ever.

"If you're trying to spare my feelings, please don't bother." Brenna tugged her wrap closer against a sudden chill. "You think it's a Seagrave."

"No proof."

Which wasn't the same thing as saying he didn't suspect one of them. But which one? If she were going to choose a family member to suspect of murder, who would it be?

Her father would have been the obvious choice, had he not been missing for so long. Eland certainly bore her enough antipathy, but where would he have gotten the money to hire an assassin? And Louise? What reason could she possibly have to invite Brenna for a visit only to have her killed? Brenna couldn't imagine, but she also couldn't shake the idea that Louise was the most likely of the three.

"Do you have a guess?" she asked hesitantly, reluctant to hear Quinn's answer.

"I do." Cryptic, and therefore completely typical of him.

"You're not going to share, are you?"

His eyes bored into hers. "Your instincts are good. What do they tell you?"

She answered without hesitation. "Louise."

Quinn very loudly said nothing.

Brenna wished she could feel shocked by his suspicions, but she didn't even feel sad. The idea was simply cold and hard, like ice around her heart.

"It will do nothing to change your assessment," she informed Quinn, "but you should know that I may have interfered with her romantic pursuit of a neighboring lord earlier today. She clearly never intended for us to meet, and now he seems to be considering transferring his attentions—to me." It proved surprisingly easy to remain emotionally detached from the information, as though she were relating distant, meaningless facts. "If I read the situation aright, Louise was hoping to convince this man that she's a wealthy widow and would make a fabulous wife for an older, impoverished peer with an estate to refurbish."

"Does he know she's not?"

"Not wealthy, or not a widow?" Brenna quipped, but sobered immediately. "I can't tell what he knows." Brenna wasn't sure whether Lord Griffin's perception was up to the task of unraveling the web of Louise's delusions. "He called us both 'Lady Seagrave' in the same breath. It doesn't seem to occur to him that it's improper for her to claim the title, so he may also not realize that she's effectively penniless. I wouldn't realize it myself if I had nothing to go on but this house."

"Is he someone you know from court?"

"Never met him before. His name is Rommel Griffin."

Brenna had the privilege of watching an actual expression appear on Quinn's face. It lasted for no more than an instant, but she thought it might have been surprise. And possibly even respect.

"You know him," she accused.

"We've met in an official capacity," Quinn confirmed.

It was Brenna's turn for surprise. "You've tried to assassinate him before?" she asked suspiciously.

"We've worked together."

Her eyes narrowed. "For Lady Norelle?"

Quinn shrugged. "She prefers not to disclose the identities of her agents, even to each other."

Outrage competed with embarrassment as Brenna recalled her performance at Lord Griffin's estate. If he was actually one of Lizbet's spies... "Well, if it's true, he now believes I'm a perfect ninny, so I doubt he suspects me of anything remotely clandestine."

But what was a Crown agent doing here? Why would he have

moved to such an out-of-the-way part of the kingdom, and be acting like a dull-witted fool, unless...

Brenna cursed under her breath. Of course. But why hadn't Lizbet told her she had someone watching Louise Seagrave? If her suspicions were that comprehensive, couldn't she have just told Brenna the truth?

The realization stung, but Brenna could guess why she hadn't. Lizbet wouldn't have wanted to poison her protégée's attempt to re-establish a relationship with her family. Especially if Lizbet's worries proved to be unfounded. But if Quinn's suspicions about his contract were true...

Brenna drew in a breath as she connected the events of the day with Faline's news, and added what she'd just learned. "And here I've been thinking Lord Griffin's wits are as agile as the average milk cow. He has someone working here. He invited us to his estate to get us out of the way while his man searched Louise's papers."

"Do you know if he found anything?"

"No." She folded her arms and scowled at the floor. And she couldn't ask Faline to investigate further. The maid would certainly do it, but it might endanger her should anyone happen to catch her snooping.

"Then I'll pay Lord Griffin a visit," Quinn said, as though he was in the habit of dropping in on lords without waiting for an invitation. Which, come to think of it, he probably was.

"Would it be too much to ask for you to terrify him at least as badly as you terrified me? He deserves it after his ridiculous performance."

"I'm an assassin," Quinn said coldly. "Not a performing monkey. And Lord Griffin isn't afraid of me."

Brenna stared at him for a moment. She had never heard him admit such a thing before. If Rom was indeed unafraid of Quinn, she would need to step cautiously indeed, though she still had every intention of paying him back for pretending to be a fool. She would simply have to do so carefully. And have very pointed words with Lizbet once she returned to Evenleigh.

"Very well," she said with a sigh. "No terrifying Lord Griffin. What ought I do while I'm waiting for news?"

"Disappear."

Wait, what?

"What do you mean, disappear?" she asked incredulously. "I can't disappear. I have a maid and a carriage. They're difficult to hide. If you want me to go home, just say so."

"If you try to leave by any of the normal methods, I believe you'll find that one of your carriage wheels was removed for repair only a few hours ago and your driver isn't feeling well."

As excuses, they sounded implausible. As reality...

"You're not making this up, are you?" A surge of pure outrage scorched through Brenna's veins and left her seething. "If I grant you that these are most likely not coincidence, I still don't understand the reasons. What does she gain from my death? Why invite me here only to kill me in a way that throws the greatest possible suspicion on her?"

"According to my instructions, you are meant to die fleeing the estate," Quinn said flatly.

Brenna thought about that. "So she invites me here in order to establish that she's just trying to be a caring mother, then irritates me beyond all reason so that I want to leave. She makes it impossible for me to depart by carriage, leaving me open to all manner of accidents that can be made to look entirely natural."

Quinn didn't answer, which was just as good as a nod from anyone else.

"Why not just have me killed in Evenleigh?"

"Too many questions. Witnesses."

That much was true. Had Brenna suddenly turned up dead at Evenburg, Lady Norelle would have moved mountains to uncover the reason.

"But we still have the question of motive," she went on doggedly. "What does she stand to gain from all of this? If I die, the estate passes to Kyril, not to her."

"The presence of Lord Griffin indicates that Lady Norelle is likewise concerned with Louise's motives."

Brenna tapped a toe on the floor. "But Lord Griffin was assigned before I became involved at all. Before Louise even sent my invitation. He must be investigating something else. Is it her money? There's certainly far more of it in this place than anyone knew she had access to." As far as Brenna could tell, none of it made any sense. "I still don't understand why she didn't have me killed somewhere else and avoid suspicion entirely. She hired the best. Doesn't she trust you?"

"No one who hires an assassin is complacent enough to trust one," Quinn answered flatly. "And she would have been questioned no matter where you died."

"So she thought it better to establish her goodwill first?" Brenna couldn't help rolling her eyes. "Look, you've already indicated you don't have proof, so all of this is just conjecture. We can't accuse her of anything, and if we're going to find evidence of guilt, we'll need her to try again. What good does it do me to disappear?"

"My instructions indicated a preference that you die in an accident," Quinn said. "In the forest."

"So if I leave, she'll assume I'm dead and possibly tip her hand," Brenna mused.

"It also rules out any other direct attempts once she realizes I've failed her. In this case, I wouldn't hesitate to expect poison."

Brenna shivered in spite of herself. How was she having a conversation about potentially being poisoned by her mother? And why wasn't she making more of an effort to protest that Louise could still be innocent?

"What about Faline?" was the only protest she could muster. "I can hide effectively enough, but she's no spy, and two people are harder to conceal than one."

"Leave her here," Quinn said.

"I will not leave my maid to Louise's revenge," Brenna snapped, outraged at his callousness. "Faline is a friend, and I do not abandon my friends."

Quinn looked bored. "She'll be in no danger, especially if she has no idea where you've gone. A second death would cause too much scrutiny."

Brenna stared at him. "What do you mean she'll have no idea where I've gone?"

He didn't respond.

"You mean now, don't you? You want me to crawl out that window right this minute and disappear into the night."

"Is that a problem?" Trust Quinn to take a poke at her professional pride.

"No, but it's terribly inconvenient and I think I hate you a little right now."

"Most people do." Another man might have looked hurt, but Quinn's face didn't even twitch. "I'll see you out to the road and then you're on your own. Your maid will be told that you're well after she's established her innocence. Once I've met with Lord Griffin, I'll find you and let you know whenever it's safe for you to resume your usual activities."

"And do you anticipate that moment coming soon, sir?" Brenna grumbled, as she moved towards the wardrobe and began digging through it, throwing things she might need into a pile on the floor.

"That will depend on Lord Griffin."

"I'm not sure I approve of Lord Griffin being in any way responsible for my future," she muttered, knowing it probably wasn't fair, but reluctant to relinquish so much control over her own life. How could she be certain he would be careful and thorough in his search for evidence? How could she trust that he wouldn't leave her in the dark for days, wondering what was happening and whether someone still wanted her dead?

"Lady Norelle trusts him."

"But what if he isn't able to find any evidence or motive, for this or anything else?"

Quinn shrugged. "Then that's up to Lady Norelle."

Her head still out of sight in the wardrobe, Brenna rolled her eyes. The man was just as impossible as she remembered.

"You're not making this any easier, Quinn. How far do I need to go?"

"Doesn't matter. I'll still find you."

She jerked her head out of the wardrobe. "So sure, are you? What if I decide I'm fed up with this whole countessing business and run away to... I don't know, Erath or something? I bet Mr. Delaney at least would be glad to see me."

"Unless he's found a new Mrs. Delaney," Quinn said dryly, in the closest Brenna had ever heard him come to humor.

"Fine." She grabbed a bag and began stuffing her chosen articles into it, finishing with a comb and her cosmetics off the bureau. Stepping behind the dressing screen, she donned a plain bodice and skirt, with breeches underneath. Faline had thoughtfully packed her favorite boots, so once she tied them up, stuffed a knife down each one and tied her hair up in a scarf, she was ready.

"Any last words of wisdom?"

"Don't let assassins into your room."

Brenna actually chuckled. "I can't believe I used to think you didn't have a sense of humor. You really do, it's just so bizarre that most people mistake your jokes for threats on their lives."

Quinn didn't even blink. "I never joke about my job."

"In that case, I'll be sure to lock my windows in the near future. Thank you for the warning, and if anything happens to Faline, I promise I will hold you personally responsible and take any damages out on your person, assassin or no."

"Duly noted." The irritating man moved towards the window. "Do you require further assistance?"

"I'm a spy, Quinn, whether or not you choose to forget it. Do you really think I need help getting out a window?"

Something that was almost a smile crossed his face. "Until next time then." He disappeared in the space of a blink and Brenna found herself letting out a long breath of both irritation and... relief. She was deeply, embarrassingly relieved.

Not by Quinn's absence—she had been oddly happy to see him. No, she was relieved to be climbing out a window in the dead of night, on her way to who knew where, to take up some sort of haphazard life until she could learn the truth of who had hired Quinn to kill her. All the while keeping her eye out for further assassination attempts and supporting herself in a strange place where she knew no one at all.

As she made her way carefully to the ground, Brenna considered the possibilities. It was going to have to be Camber, at least to start. Once there, she could reconsider her options and weigh the dangers of staying close with the desire to obtain information on her own.

It was eight miles to Camber, but Brenna had never been afraid of a little walking. Walking in the dark? That didn't scare her either. Especially not through the densely wooded countryside. Out there was nothing to fear but wild things, creatures that would much prefer to leave her alone. Had it been the city? That would have been another thing entirely. Humans were far more terrifying predators than anything that lurked beneath the trees.

Those eight miles would also give her time to decide what she wanted to do, and who she wanted to be. She'd had more fake identities than some girls had dresses, and tried her hand at a number of unusual jobs. If she decided to stay, Camber was large enough that she should be able to find something, though small enough that it would be difficult to truly disappear.

A challenge! As Brenna set off through the shadows, a thrill of excitement shot through her and a grin crossed her lips. She hadn't had this much fun in ages. The real danger was not so much that someone might try to kill her—she was rather hoping they would. The bigger problem was that she might enjoy it too much to want to go back.

CHAPTER 6

*D*ear Sir,

Please inform me of your success or failure at your earliest convenience or I shall be forced to consider this matter unresolved. Might I remind you that your terms have been met and your fee has been promptly paid? While I congratulate you on managing the matter of your target's disappearance, the lack of proof of your complete and final success is unacceptable. I should hardly need to explain to a professional of your reputation that a few drops of blood on the carpet cannot be considered evidence of anything. If I have not received an explanation of either your progress or your future plans within three days, you may find it difficult to obtain further contracts.

- Grim Hill

Rom stalked across his study, wearing a path from the desk to the window as he seethed with fear and no small amount of fury. A message had arrived, early, from Crestwood, with strange and disturbing information—Lady Seagrave was missing from the house and presumed dead.

Her driver had been found ill and nearly unconscious in the carriage house. One of her carriage wheels, which had been removed for repair, was nowhere to be found. And then there was the tiny matter of her maid, who had succumbed to violent hysterics when she discovered bloodstains on the floor of her mistress's room.

All of it pointed to foul play, and Rom didn't feel the need to guess at who might be responsible. But he still had no proof. Danward had come up with nothing during his search of Louise's study, and reported in his hastily dashed-off note that his mistress had apparently fallen into a dead faint at the news of her daughter's disappearance and evident murder.

If Louise had indeed been responsible, Rom might very well end up blaming himself. If he hadn't flirted with the daughter, giving the older woman the idea that her pursuit of him was hopeless, she would most likely have never stooped to such a violent act. And poor Lady Seagrave—the young countess was so guileless, she would have been caught entirely by surprise by any violence against her person. She wouldn't have stood a chance against her mother's machinations, and Rom should have had the sense to warn her.

If she would have had the sense to listen, which he doubted.

He was staring out the window when he became aware that someone else was in his study. It wasn't the sound—the person was incredibly stealthy—but the feeling of presence. As if the room was no longer as empty as it should have been. Rom considered the likely points of entry and determined that the intruder had probably been there since before his own arrival.

"If you have something to say, I would appreciate your brevity. I prefer to pace without an audience."

"Well done, Lord Griffin."

Rom turned to see a familiar sandy-haired man perched on the edge of his desk as though he owned it.

"Quinn. Testing me, or testing yourself?"

"Can a man not do both?"

"I would ask what brings you here, but I can guess."

"Lady Seagrave."

"Older or younger?"

Quinn shot him a cool glance. "There's only one."

That was interesting. Somehow, Quinn was already a partisan in this fight. Or perhaps he was merely a stickler for the finer points of the law. "You know where she is?"

"No." Quinn stood and joined him at the window. "But I know I was hired to kill her."

Rom took a step back, every hair on his body standing on end, and firmly denied himself the pleasure of reaching for a weapon. "And did you?"

Quinn's raised eyebrow was answer enough.

"You don't know who hired you, do you?"

"Not yet. The messenger was traced to Camber. Lady Norelle has tasked me with finding out who paid him before further action is taken. If Louise Seagrave is at fault, the evidence must be clear. Beyond all doubt."

Rom grunted and walked back to his desk. "I've been here for months and haven't managed to find conclusive evidence of anything else she's suspected of. No money trail, no communication with Thalassa, no suspicious visitors. What makes Lady Norelle think that will change?"

The shorter man cast him an inscrutable glance. "I understand the former Lady Seagrave has designs on you."

Rom felt a flush rising and tugged at his collar. "Who told you that?"

"The current Lady Seagrave. She seemed quite certain that Louise hopes to convince you to marry her for her money."

"Then Lady Seagrave is far more observant than she seems," Rom said dryly. "Though I can't quite picture her having a rational conversation with an assassin."

Quinn said nothing, so Rom let the matter drop.

"I knew Louise was flirting," he admitted, "but it honestly never occurred to me that she might be serious enough to commit murder over it." Rom shook his head incredulously. "I know I look older than I am, but she's what... over twelve years my senior? Even if she were as rich as she pretends, what man would be tempted?"

"One who believed she could offer him status as well as wealth, and might be dazzled by a refined, mature woman," Quinn said.

"You mean an idiot such as Rommel Griffin is currently pretending to be?"

Thankfully, Quinn ignored the opportunity to needle him. "She needs stability. Craves recognition. Her husband has been missing over a year, which means their marriage can be legally dissolved by Andari law if she chooses. You're a fool with a title, you don't seem desperate for an heir, and her estate neighbors yours. Why wouldn't you be tempted by a rich widow who could enlarge your holdings, and who used to have connections at court?"

It was the longest speech he'd ever heard Quinn make. It also had the ring of truth.

"Even so, why would Louise invite her daughter here, where Brenna's death could only invite scrutiny? Why not have her quietly murdered in Evenleigh?"

"Lady Seagrave knows too many important people," Quinn pointed out, surprising Rom. "Her death in Evenleigh would immediately be considered suspicious and investigated accordingly."

"And it won't here?"

"It was meant to look like an accident." Quinn shrugged. "Also, the former countess may have wished to establish her innocence by demonstrating her desire to connect with Brenna now that the earl is out of the picture."

If it was true, the old witch got more than she bargained for. First an afternoon of utter embarrassment, and then her intended target's disappearance.

Rom grunted his assent. "So have you seen her?"

"Louise?"

"Lady Seagrave," Rom corrected impatiently. "You apparently staged her murder so effectively that Louise fainted and her maid is having hysterics."

"I told her to disappear."

"You told..." Rom got hold of himself with an effort. "You've met Lady Seagrave, correct?"

"Yes." Quinn remained impassive.

"And you just let her wander off with the instruction to disappear? The woman is likely to end up in a hole in the middle of the woods being mauled to death by skunks!"

The prospect didn't seem to concern the other man in the slightest. "If you're so worried, why don't you go find her?"

"Dash it all, Quinn!" Rom ran a hand through his hair and grabbed his jacket off the arm of his chair. "I'm involved in an investigation at the moment. I don't have time to chase runaway heiresses."

"Then leave her be."

Rom shot the assassin a frustrated glare. "I can't. Lady Norelle explicitly charged me with keeping an eye on her, and if anything happens while she's here, it's my head on a pike, not yours."

As he strode out of his office, Quinn called after him.

"I wouldn't suggest trying to rescue her."

"Why not?" Rom turned back with a scowl.

"She won't like it." Quinn's expression was unreadable.

"Then she shouldn't run off and get lost! As it stands, I've got no choice but to find her before she gets into who knows what kind of trouble."

Quinn's lips curved into a smile. It was not a happy look, more the expression of something dangerous, hungry, and very, very amused.

"Good luck," he said.

~

On her first morning in Camber, Brenna visited an apothecary shop and a store selling ready-made clothing. Afterwards, she returned to her hotel room, which she'd acquired only by claiming to be a maid preparing for her mistress's arrival. Hotels did not generally permit unattached and unchaperoned young women to rent rooms, so she would only be allowed to remain for as long as it took them to realize that her "mistress" was never going to arrive.

A few hours later, she emerged feeling like an entirely different person. If she had done her work well, the rest of the world would have to agree. Her hair had been dyed to an unrelieved black, and her clothes were now that of a just barely respectable female from the seedier side of town. A red bodice was laced tightly over a plain white blouse, while her dark skirt featured enough flounces to catch the eye. High-heeled boots completed the outfit, leaving Brenna quite ready to set out in search of gainful employment, and, hopefully, a more permanent place to live.

During her years working for Lady Norelle, Brenna had held numerous jobs, but one of her favorites was the time she'd spent as a tavern keeper. After a few drinks, a mark would tell a tavernkeep nearly anything, especially if she was female and sympathetic. The food was usually decent, the company was rarely pretentious, and no one expected her to fake anything. When she was hungry, she ate. When she was angry, she'd occasionally punched a man in the face and found herself congratulated for doing so. If anyone got drunk, she simply threw them out. Men would come in for a pint and a chat, but they usually kept their hands to themselves and then went home to their families, while those who didn't have families might stay until closing time.

She'd found it to be simple, satisfying work, and, as a bonus, no one acquainted with the Countess of Hennsley would ever think to look for her in a seedy pub.

Sadly, no one in Camber seemed to be hiring. Brenna traipsed from one tavern to another until she was exhausted and her feet hurt, but it was clear that not only was she in a much smaller town than she was used to, they didn't much care for outsiders. At one place she'd actually had a fish thrown at her when she didn't leave fast enough after her request for employment was rejected.

It was growing late, and Brenna was beginning to think she needed a new plan. She'd never had this much trouble finding work before. Maybe the hotel would let her stay another night, and she could try a different appearance and a different sort of business the next day. There might be a higher demand for bookkeepers, which would make it providential that Brenna had remembered to pack her most sensible and respectable outfit when she was fleeing Crestwood in such unseemly haste.

But when she returned to the hotel, the first thing she noticed was her bag, already packed, lying on the floor just to the side of the desk. She caught the eye of the clerk, who merely sniffed and held out a hand for her key, never deigning to so much as speak to her.

Apparently they'd discovered her deception sooner than she'd hoped.

Brenna handed over the key, shouldered her bag, trudged back into the street, and headed for a less affluent part of town.

There were a few pubs she hadn't tried yet, mostly because they appeared to be the sort that wouldn't necessarily welcome women. She'd worked at a few before, and it was always more of a challenge to prove that she could handle herself and wouldn't tolerate disrespect.

And there were some she wouldn't even walk into because it was simply too dangerous.

After surveying the last available options, Brenna decided to start with The Bad Apple. She'd passed it by before because it was loud, crowded, and right in the middle of the busiest street in the area. It also had a laughably awful sign featuring what appeared to be an ancient crone holding a piece of fruit, but it wasn't like Brenna was in a position to be choosy.

After taking a moment to assess the crowd, Brenna pushed through the doors and took her time strolling up to the bar. She cast an assessing eye over the patrons, and even bestowed a wink on one or two, noting that they were overwhelmingly male. It had already become apparent that in Camber, women did not frequent pubs for their own amusement.

Quite gratifyingly, conversation slowed for a moment as the customers eyed her back before returning to their drinks. They appeared to have pegged her as unusual but ultimately forgettable —which meant her disguise was perfect.

Interestingly, the bar was currently being tended by a woman.

"You must be new around here," the nasal-voiced brunette called from behind the bar. "Let me acquaint you with the way of things. If you're lookin' for a dance hall, this isn't it. If you're lookin' for a free meal, this isn't a charity. And if you're lookin' for a man, I think he ran out the back way when he saw you coming."

The crowd roared with laughter, and Brenna grinned right along with them, feeling suddenly quite at home. This was a game she knew how to play.

"If I were looking for a man," she returned with a wink, "he'd be under the table, wetting himself and pleading for mercy. But as it happens, I'm looking for a job. I work all hours, I don't spill unless the customer deserves it, and I don't stand any nonsense. I can sing, dance, cook and clean, but if a man touches me without my permission, he loses a hand. Any chance you'd happen to be needing an experienced barmaid?"

The woman behind the bar looked at her and snorted. "Experienced, are you? If you've that much experience, why ha'nt you got a job? Do you even know the proper way to be waterin' down a beer on a bad night?"

Brenna let a bit of ice show in her eyes. "Perhaps I've made a mistake in coming in here. I've always been honest, and I'd never work for a 'keep, man or woman, who would water down their beer and charge the same for it." She started to turn away.

"Very good then. But what do you do when the customers are drunk and ready to riot?"

Brenna sensed rather than saw the man approaching her from behind, right before she smelled his breath. She'd rather hoped she could irritate a regular into trying something, but it was kind of him to time his interruption so beautifully. When his hand latched onto her arm and spun her around, she grinned.

"This," she said, pulling free and linking arms with the startled drunk, only to grab his wrist and twist it up behind his back until he began to howl. "Now this nice fellow will do anything I ask, just so long as I promise not to break his wrist. Won't you?" She pressed a little harder, and the man shrieked.

"All right, all right, let him go." The disgruntled barkeep waved a towel at her. "Petey, sit down, man, before she takes your arm off." She eyed Brenna with a bit less hostility. "Happens I could use you. My best muscle is laid up with a broken leg, so if you can serve and stop the rascals from starting fights, I might pay extra."

Brenna concealed her sigh of relief, walked back to the bar and held out a hand to seal the deal. "I appreciate you giving me a chance. My name's Renee, and I've just arrived in town. Would you happen to know of a boarding house that takes single women?"

The other woman chuckled. "Camber's not so big as that. Mayhap they have such a thing in places like Lansbridge, but folk are a bit more old-fashioned in these parts."

Brenna let her face fall, and it wasn't much of an act. She had no idea where she could stay now that the hotel had kicked her out. "What do your other girls do?"

"Oh, they're all married, or living at home."

"I suppose they're lucky to have the option."

"Some of 'em, maybe." She eyed Brenna. "You married?"

"Never met a man I cared to take home. Most of 'em seem too much like my da, and that's more than I ever cared to put up with."

The other woman chuckled. "Fair enough. Look, Renee, if you think you'll be staying a while, I may have an idea. A few friends have a place of their own a few streets over, but they're careful about who they accept. You'd have to pay your own way, keep your space clean, and contribute to the household chores, though none of them can cook, so the food won't be anything to brag about. I'd live with them myself, but I look after my ma and we do all right together."

"Your ma is lucky," Brenna said sincerely.

The woman grunted, but she didn't appear displeased. "Go two streets to the south, look for the place with a fence. Not much to brag of on the outside, but it's clean enough. Ask for Grita, and tell her Myra sent you."

"My thanks." Brenna nodded. "When would you like me to start?"

"How about tomorrow?"

Brenna grinned. It might not have been her first choice, but working at The Bad Apple just might be the most fun she'd had in a long time.

It didn't take long for Brenna to explore the neighborhood Myra indicated, eventually locating the run-down little house with a fence around the front. It was tucked in between two much taller buildings, and the roof appeared to have been slapped on at an odd angle, but it was clean, the yard was neat, and there were curtains over the tiny front window.

She went through the gate, noted the well-swept walk, and knocked firmly on the green-painted door.

After a few moments, it cracked open to reveal a baleful dark eye.

"What do you want?" a gruff female voice demanded.

"Are you Grita?" Brenna tried her best to sound friendly and non-threatening. "My name is Renee. Myra sent me. She said you might be willing to take on another single female boarder."

"No." The door slammed.

Brenna's heart sank, but she knocked again.

"Go away."

"I can't. There's nowhere else in town that will rent me a room."

"Then there's just nowhere. I don't rent rooms to anyone I don't know."

"Please give me a chance." She didn't like to beg, but she liked sleeping in the street even less. "I pay well, I clean up after myself, and I know how to cook."

The door swung open a crack. "You said Myra sent you? What can you cook?"

Brenna shrugged. "Yes, and tavern fare, mostly. Soups, stews, bread, biscuits, and pies. Apple pie is my specialty, but my meat pies are good too."

The door opened a little wider, revealing a tall brunette wearing what appeared to be a habitual scowl. "You'd have to abide by all our rules if you want to live here. No men are allowed in the house, ever. You lose your job, you tell us. You decide to move on, you tell us. You nose into anyone else's business or ask too many questions, you're out. We all have our secrets and we keep them."

"Sounds perfect." Actually, it sounded awful, but Brenna wasn't in a position to object. "When can I move in?"

Grita stepped back to reveal a narrow hallway. "Come in and meet the others. They'll have to decide if anyone's willing to share a room with you."

She led the way to a cramped, dingy room with a single fireplace, where six other women were clustered around a small table, engaged in various tasks.

"All right, pay attention," Grita said, her arms folded tightly across her chest. "This is Renee. She's new in town, she needs a place, and she cooks. Anyone care to throw her out?"

The chorus of replies was immediate and decisively affirmative.

"Please stay!" said a cheerful blonde woman with a smattering of freckles over her nose. "I'm Hannah, by the way, and we'd love to have you."

Brenna was relieved to find that not all the women were as unfriendly as Grita.

"Anything but your cooking, Grita love," joked a tall redhead. She offered Brenna a quirky grin. "I'm Sinna."

"Does she do windows?" That was from a loose-limbed girl of maybe sixteen, who drew a quelling look from the much older Grita.

"That's enough, Dora." She glared around the room and

nodded once. "Fine. She stays. Everyone else give their names and decide who's sharing."

Brenna was quickly introduced to Silvie, Dulcie, and Batrice. Aside from Grita, the women all appeared to be quite a bit younger than Brenna. They also, unlike Grita, all seemed to have a sense of humor. Dora, the youngest, was the least serious, and the only one who volunteered to share a room.

"It's tiny," she said apologetically, "but there's enough space for another bed."

"Thank you for letting me stay." Brenna had never felt a more sincere sense of relief and gratitude. They had no reason to trust her, and probably more reason than most to turn her away, but they hadn't.

The situation was odd enough that Brenna wished she could ask these women for their stories, but Grita had made it clear that questions were strictly forbidden. For now she would simply have to prove that she was worthy of their trust.

Even if she really wasn't. Not when she was using their home as a place to hide from someone who wanted to kill her. It caused her a twinge of guilt, but Brenna reasoned that Quinn would never actually hurt any of them, and if Louise *had* been the one to hire him, the former countess would hesitate before causing harm to anyone but Brenna. The other women should be in no danger.

She hoped.

"So, where do you work?" Batrice seemed to be the most

outgoing of the lot. She was also the only one who was dressed more outrageously than Brenna herself.

"I've just convinced Myra to take me on at The Bad Apple."

Dora giggled adorably, revealing a dimple in one cheek. "As what?" she asked.

"Bouncer," Brenna replied, straight faced.

A chorus of laughter ensued, from everyone but Grita.

"No, really, are you a barmaid?" Batrice asked curiously.

"Something like that," Brenna admitted. "What about you?"

"Oh, I'm an actress." Batrice flopped down onto the single couch in the room with a dramatic sigh. "And an acrobat on occasion."

That explained the short, sparkling skirt and tightly fitting pants beneath it.

"I'm out of work at the moment," she continued, "on account of me being so shy and retiring."

The other women chuckled, and one of them chucked a cushion at her.

Batrice grinned and threw it back. "There aren't many roles for women," she admitted. "I was with a troupe of traveling performers for a few years, but it wasn't really what you'd call a steady job."

"Sounds like an exciting life," Brenna remarked, "if you enjoy seeing new places."

"I did." Batrice shrugged. "Anything was better than sitting around in drawing rooms being dull and decorative. At least until the owner of the traveling company insisted that I marry him if I wanted to stay on. I'm only here while I wait for a better opportunity."

Brenna was already considering what Lizbet might make of an acrobatic actress with a taste for travel, but suspended her speculation when Batrice continued her introductions.

"Grita sells flowers," she said, grinning unrepentantly when the older woman shot her a scowl. "Which explains her sunny personality. Sinna is allergic to flowers, and works as an apothecary's assistant, which means she can cure you or poison you, and we all hope she doesn't ever get confused about which is which." She leaned closer to Brenna and whispered loudly, "We don't let her cook!"

Sinna laughed merrily and Brenna couldn't help but join in.

"Dulcie is a copyist for a bookseller, and can teach you to read if you don't already know."

The bespectacled Dulcie blushed bright red. "Batrice, I'm sure Renee can read."

Batrice only shrugged, unrepentant. "You never know. Dora is a waitress like you, but she works at a fancy hotel and serves sandwiches to handsome gentlemen in expensive coats, so she's hoping someday one of them will take a fancy to her sandwich-serving skills and sweep her off to his mansion."

"Aye, after which I'll invite you all to live with me in luxury, eating sweets and not getting out of bed until luncheon every day," Dora said, giving a dreamy sigh and fluttering her lashes.

Brenna suppressed a sigh of her own at the young woman's naive dreams. Living in luxury was not all she'd once believed it to be. And as for being swept off her feet...Well, she hoped Dora would find someone someday who would do just that. And who would care for her genuinely and completely, without regard to her face, her money, or her family.

"That leaves Silvie and Hannah," Batrice said. "Hannah takes in sewing. She can let down a dress faster than anyone I've ever seen, works until her fingers bleed and almost never takes any time for herself, and yet somehow still doesn't have any idea how to frown."

"I can too!" Hannah protested, pulling her lips into a crooked grimace and crossing her eyes until everyone in the room, including her, began to laugh.

"And finally," Batrice concluded, "you should know that Silvie is a laundress. She gets up so early that she's usually yawning by dinnertime, but she's a genius at removing even the most appalling stains, including blood, so if you ever feel inclined to commit murder, you'll want her on your side."

"I'll keep that in mind," Brenna said with a dry chuckle. "I had to clean up from all my previous murders by myself."

Hannah looked up from the stocking she was mending. "So where are you from, Renee? Have you been in town long?" Brenna began to suspect that the rule against questions was Grita's alone, as none of the other ladies seemed to have anything against sharing secrets.

"Oh, I've been around," Brenna said vaguely. "But my last job was in Evenleigh."

Another chorus of questions arose. Everyone wanted to know what it was like, if she had ever been to the palace, if she had ever seen either of the princes, and whether Princess Trystan was beautiful.

Laughing, Brenna tried to field their questions without giving away too much about her past. "I have seen Prince Ramsey," she admitted, "and Princess Trystan too. They aren't exactly the handsome prince and beautiful princess of storybooks, but they are kind and very popular with the people of Evenleigh. I believe they care about Andar very much, and, from what I hear, they are also very much in love."

A chorus of sighs echoed around the room. "Is it true she's a commoner?" Dora asked.

"Her father was a landowner, with a peerage," Brenna told her regretfully. "But she spent much of her life believing she was illegitimate, and the prince loved her anyway." She probably shouldn't encourage them, but what was life without dreams of the future?

Was that why she felt so dissatisfied of late? For years, all of her dreams for the future had been of acceptance by her family. Of finally taking the place she'd been born to. Now she had that place, and the prize was both empty and bitter. Everything she'd once loved about her life was gone, so what did she have left to dream of now?

Before she could sink too deeply into that train of thought, the other women began to open up and share their own histories. All were from poor families except Batrice, and most had left their homes hoping to achieve some degree of financial independence, in defiance of their families' preferences. That was always a hard road for a woman alone, but somehow, these seven women had all found each other and banded together.

They were all so different, and yet in some way, each of them reminded Brenna of her own past. They may have chosen this path, while she had been forced onto it by necessity, but their stories were echoes of the road she'd walked to get to where she was.

For Grita, Dulcie, Batrice, and the others, that road was unlikely to end with a fortune and a title. But none of them seemed unhappy with their choices—there was joy and contentment in that little house, and a feeling of community that made Brenna ache to find such a thing for herself, and not for only a few days under an assumed name.

That night, as Brenna lay on a narrow cot in a tiny room, listening to the deep, even breaths of Dora only a short distance away, she wondered whether she would change her past, if she had the chance. Knowing what she now knew of her family—their prejudices and their entitlement—would she choose to be raised as a part of it for the sake of security, or choose to remain Brenna Haverly, who worked hard to provide for herself and hadn't always known where home was? Would she still wish to be accepted by her family if it meant taking back all those years of figuring out how to stand on her own, to make her own choices and be responsible for her own future?

No.

Brenna took a deep breath and allowed a few tears to escape as she realized she should actually be grateful for the life she'd been granted. She'd once resented her parents for abandoning her to an uncertain fate—for forcing her to grow up in a home for orphaned girls with no one who cared what became of her.

But it had spared her from a far worse fate. From growing up surrounded by a cold, uncaring family, learning nothing of warmth or love, unable to engage in something so simple as friendship without layer upon layer of calculation and deception. From growing into a woman like her mother.

Instead, she'd lived a life of hard work and fought for her independence. She'd gained the confidence to acquire new skills, approach the unknown with curiosity, and go after the things she wanted.

And like the women whose house she now shared, she'd done it with the help of others like herself. Other strong women who had taken the place of the mother she'd never known. Like Miss Prentiss, who had taught her to keep accounts and given her a chance to use her mind. And Lady Norelle, who had believed in Brenna enough to offer her countless opportunities to grow and learn and try new things without fear of failure.

Staring into the dark, Brenna swore to herself in that moment that if she ever had a daughter, that daughter would never have to leave her family in order to reach for her dreams. She would have loving parents who encouraged her to become as strong as she dared, and supported her in whatever course she set for herself. And she would never, ever, be made to feel smaller to increase her own mother's consequence.

Too bad there was really no point in speculating about children she didn't and probably never would have. For now, all Brenna really needed to do was survive the day ahead. And then the day after that. And the day after that. After experiencing the suffocating life of a countess, taking each day as it came seemed like a blessed relief.

Because when it was over, she would have to go home. Back to her life of suffocating privilege and smiling, cold-eyed lies. The world that had formed Louise Seagrave's character.

Perhaps Brenna ought not wonder how her mother could have become so cold and cruel, but rather wonder how any of the nobility escaped that fate.

CHAPTER 7

*D*ear Sir,

  Taking into account your status as a professional of impeccable reputation, I can only consider your performance thus far to be utterly lacking. If you recall, it was suggested that an accident in the forest was to be preferred, as it simplifies disposal and prevents immediate discovery. As it is, the thing is bungled nearly beyond repair. If I do not receive word of your success by this evening, consider our association at an end.

- Grim Hill

Rom stalked down the streets of Camber feeling utterly annoyed with the world. Three days he'd searched the woods near Louise Seagrave's estate, enduring mud, brambles and an encounter with a seriously annoyed bear. On the first day, it had rained for the entire afternoon and his horse had thrown a shoe, forcing him to walk back to Lorenhall. On the second, he'd twisted his ankle falling into a whistler's burrow, and on the third, a pair of vagrants had made an ill-considered attempt to relieve him of his coat and boots.

After all that, he'd found nothing but aggravation and confusion. He had certainly found no trace of the slightly silly Lady Seagrave, whom everyone but he and Quinn seemed convinced was dead.

Perhaps he was the fool for believing otherwise, but according to the only note he'd received from Danward since that fateful night, the only proof of foul play had been a few drops of blood on the carpet, which Quinn had admitted to leaving for the servants to find. He'd insisted they were necessary to produce a genuine reaction from Lady Seagrave's maid, and to hopefully provoke an entirely different sort of reaction from whoever had hired him.

Despite the lack of convincing evidence, Louise had donned black and insisted her entire household do the same. She maintained that something terrible must have happened and that it was all her fault, a fact which Rom was in no mood to dispute, even to be polite.

If he didn't find the errant countess soon, he would be forced to send a message to Lady Norelle, and that was not an action he cared to take. For whatever reason, she was clearly fond of the vapid and tactless Lady Seagrave, and Rom winced whenever he thought of his employer's response should he be forced to admit that he'd lost her.

Where could she have gone? And how could she have disappeared leaving no evidence behind? Granted, she hadn't been a countess forever, so she knew something of the world, but to the best of his knowledge, the current Lady Seagrave had grown up in the city. She would have been terrified to be alone in the woods at night, and even if she'd survived that and made her way to Camber, she'd be alone in a strange town with no money and no friends.

Was it possible that Louise was right, and she truly was dead?

Rom decided to hunt down some of his local contacts. He'd made several casual acquaintances on the shadier side of Camber society since moving to town, and they typically kept him apprised of any happenings he might find of interest. Sadly, it had been a while since they'd convened over a pint, but as long as he was willing to buy the beer, they would no doubt be happy to renew the relationship. He was counting on the fact that someone who stood out as badly as Lady Seagrave was bound to have made a stir in a town like Camber, and someone, somewhere, would be gossiping about it.

Over the course of the evening, he made his way around to several of his favorite local spots, but no matter how many drinks he bought, no one seemed to have heard or seen anything. They were happy to accept free beer, but it accomplished nothing beyond acquainting him with the usual selection of well-worn local legends and personal marital woes.

Rom was beginning to consider simply buying the drinks for himself when he stepped into yet another tavern full of loud, boisterous, excessively cheerful people. He wasn't sure how many more of these he could take. The Bad Apple was particularly crowded, and he had to clench his teeth against the onset of a headache as he shoved his way as politely as possible through the crush to reach the bar.

He'd only made it halfway when his progress was stopped by the beginnings of a shoving match between overenthusiastic patrons. Before it could devolve into an out-and-out rip-roaring bar fight, however, it was interrupted by a firm hand. Two hands really, one pinching an ear of each of the offenders.

"And that'll be enough of that. Grint, Delber, you either keep those hands to yourselves or I'll be pouring your drinks into your boots and returning you to your wives smelling of ale and wet socks, is that clear?"

It was a woman. The crowd roared with laughter as the two men sagged in her grip and muttered their apologies. Rom, however, was entirely engaged in staring at the apparition before him.

She was new, that was for sure. He would have remembered if he'd seen her before. The woman with a rather hairy ear in each hand was not particularly tall, despite the fact that she wore boots with impressively high heels. She wasn't even all that terrifying to look at—she was actually quite pretty—but her sense of fashion was decidedly startling. She wore a flounced skirt that cut away in front to reveal trousers tucked into her boots, a tightly laced red bodice over a white silk blouse, and about twenty bracelets on each arm. Her enormous blue eyes were outlined dramatically in black, and a kerchief wrapped around only enough of her head to prevent her long black hair from falling into the customers' drinks.

Rom stared a little too long. She looked up from the altercation at hand, caught his eye, and winked. "Hello there, love. What can I get you?"

And that's when Rom finally realized he was looking into the eyes of Brenna Seagrave, Countess of Hennsley, who was clearly enjoying herself, and was most decidedly not dead.

"You…" he spluttered, but she interrupted him before he could decide what sort of words would be appropriate to the situation.

"Pardon me," she said with a smile, and turned away to drop the two would-be wrestlers back in their seats.

"Now"—she turned back, eyes gleaming—"I'd be happy to get you a drink, but, as I've not seen you here before, I'll warn you of the rules. We don't stand for any language and if you harass the barmaids I'll not hesitate to throw you into the street. It's all very well for the likes of you to want to mingle with the common folk, but we don't have to put up with any of your unsavory habits."

"My… unsavory habits?" Rom growled softly, feeling his jaw grow dangerously tense. "I've been searching the blasted woods for you for three days. *Three days.* Not to mention buying drinks for half of Camber in hopes someone remembered seeing you. And you're here playing barkeep without a care in the world like..."

"And you can just shut your lips before you go any further," Brenna said, her voice turning to steel. "Whatever you were about to say, I don't care, but you won't be insulting working girls in front of me."

"I wasn't insulting anyone, you infuriating woman! I was about to say that you're not just an ordinary person who can afford to disappear. You have obligations and responsibilities and people who care about you, though at the moment I honestly can't imagine why. What were you thinking, endangering yourself this way?"

Her eyes narrowed ominously and Rom thought about taking a step back, but he was just a moment too late.

"And here's another one with a bit too big of a mouth on 'im," she called out, above the noise of the crowd. "Shall I throw him out?"

A loud cheer answered her, and the sound was mostly affirmative.

"You can't throw me out," Rom asserted.

"Maybe I *shouldn't*," she said, smirking, "but never tell me I can't."

Before it occurred to him that he might need to defend himself against a countess dressed as a barmaid, she had twisted his arm up behind his back.

"Outside," she murmured in his ear, "without another word. Maybe you don't mind if the whole town knows your business, but I don't care to share mine."

Something was very wrong. Very wrong indeed. For one thing, this woman was neither silly or helpless. She might look like Brenna Seagrave, but looks were the only thing they had in common. For another, Rom could feel what he suspected was the point of a knife resting against his kidney.

Very careful not to make any sudden moves, Rom edged out the door, followed by the woman he was beginning to think hadn't wanted to be found.

As soon as he shuffled around the corner and into the alley, Brenna released his wrist and shoved him a few steps away from her. Sure enough, when he turned around, he could see the cold glint of a knife in her hand. It was too dark to see her eyes, but he could feel the fury radiating from her whole body.

"Out of all the pubs in town, why did you have to show up at this one?" she snarled. "I was happy, and everything was fine. Now I'm going to have to explain why you think you know me, because I told them I was new here."

"You're not going to have to explain anything, because you're coming back with me," Rom ordered, barely resisting the urge to throw up his hands in exasperation.

"And why would I do that?"

"Because if anyone else finds you here, your reputation will be in tatters!"

"And how exactly would my reputation be any less tarnished if I go with you?" She retorted derisively. "How is it better for me to eventually be discovered hiding out, unchaperoned, in the home of the rather silly Lord Griffin? Who is not only a fool, but appears to be a hardened flirt and has occasionally been seen down dark alleys in the company of tavern girls!"

She might have a point, but this was no time for her to be making it. How could she not see that this was no place for a countess? Let alone that she wasn't doing a very good job of hiding when anyone and everyone could stroll past the pub and see her without even bothering to go inside.

Rom considered tearing his hair out, but it seemed more constructive to take a deep, cleansing breath. He hadn't wanted to blow his cover, not to her, but he would, if it meant keeping her safe and fulfilling his obligation to Lady Norelle.

"You should come with me," he said, hoping he sounded more patient than he felt, "because it is the particular wish of Lady Lizbet Norelle that you come to no harm while you are here. She has tasked me with ensuring that this is the case, and as I have no wish to incur her wrath, I will go to great lengths to prevent you from embroiling yourself in situations that are likely to prove dangerous. Such as, working as a *pub bouncer*, for the love of Andar!"

"So you'd have me go back to Crestwood and be murdered instead?"

"My lady, the name of your would-be assassin is Quinn, and he's not going to murder you," Rom said dryly. "It sounds as though the two of you have chatted, and I promise that real assassins rarely do that if they intend to carry out their contracts. Quinn is actually in the employ of Lady Norelle and is investigating the matter of who might have reason to target you."

Brenna actually laughed. "Quinn? Working for Lady Norelle? A bit off the mark there, aren't you? Quinn is a dear, but he works directly for the Crown. And sometimes for himself, I think. A man of his reputation can probably choose his own clients."

Quinn was a *what?* Rom found himself taken aback once more and his eyes narrowed. "How exactly do you know Quinn, Lady Seagrave? And what is Lady Norelle to you?"

"I'm afraid the answers to both of those are 'that's my business,'" Brenna replied flatly. "I'm not concerned about Quinn. What bothers me more is that no one knows for certain whether it was my dear lady mother who hired him. And if she did, we likewise have no idea what methods she's likely to employ next, once she finds out he failed."

"If you come home with me, you'll be protected," Rom insisted. "No one is going to come looking for you at my estate."

Brenna chuckled. "And if they do? A man who's pretending to be a feckless incompetent can't very well protect me, and I can't protect myself when I don't know where the threat is coming from. What if it's Louise and she's bought one of your staff? It seems you've bought one of hers, so that's not exactly out of the question."

Rom considered her, thankful for the shadows that concealed

his expression. How long had she known he was pretending? He didn't think his acting was that bad. Had Quinn told her? And how *did* a countess become acquainted with an assassin? The mysteries continued to pile up, and their quantity was beginning to irritate him.

"Are you sure you're really the Countess of Hennsley?"

The woman sighed and lowered the knife. "Why, because I'm not stupid, because I know how to break up a bar fight, or because I managed to get the best of you? Does it offend you that a countess might know how to do any of those things?"

"Not at all," Rom said hastily. "Your handling of those men in the pub was one of the most impressive things I've seen in the last ten years. If I hadn't already met you, I would have taken you for an experienced pubkeeper. But you have to admit... it's an unusual skill set for a woman of your position."

"Yes, well I have an unusual background for a woman of my position," she retorted. "And frankly, considering what most of you courtiers are like, I prefer being mistaken for a pubkeeper. At least in a pub, people insult you to your face, and if they want to fight they just hit you. They don't hire assassins, or whisper about you behind your back. And if my customers are rude and demeaning, I can just punch them in the face, instead of being forced to smile and pretend it never happened."

Rom winced at the truth of it. "I'm sorry," he said at last, and meant it. "For underestimating you, and for my rudeness. Quinn came to me a few days ago and informed me of his part in all of this, but he didn't know where you'd gone. After my impression of you at Lorenhall, I was worried that, well…"

"That I'd fallen in a roadside ditch and was waiting for a man to help me out?" Brenna inquired sweetly.

"Can you blame me?"

"Not entirely," she admitted. "Our last meeting probably wasn't my finest moment, but was it at least a convincing performance?"

Rom grinned. "Very. I was starting to wonder if you were a different woman."

She sighed, and adjusted the scarf on her hair. "I suppose I shouldn't have done it, but Mother Dearest was picking at me relentlessly. I couldn't tell whether she was just deeply disappointed in my entire person, or deliberately attempting to annoy me, but nothing I did or said was good enough for her. She was determined to present me in the worst light possible, so I set out to prove just how much worse it could be."

Rom actually found himself chuckling. "Is this where I tell you it wasn't that bad or should I congratulate you on your appalling success?"

"I prefer not to be lied to," she replied tartly. "I also prefer to succeed at my goals, even when my goal is to be perceived as an unparalleled disaster."

"And how badly did Louise respond?"

"You mean besides trying to have me murdered?" Brenna grumbled. "Barely at all. No thanks to you. She was much too upset by the abrupt transfer of your affections. I don't think she intended for us to meet at all, so when you began paying me marked attentions I believe her worst fears were realized."

He winced at the realization of the part he had played in that charade. "I suppose that didn't help. I was growing desperate to find a way to convince her that I wasn't interested."

"Yes, and that worked out so well for everyone." Brenna sounded more than a little irritated.

"I apologize for using you," Rom said, guessing at the source of her irritation. "I was only trying to dissuade her from her pursuit, but that was poorly done of me."

Brenna didn't seem quite satisfied by his apology. "But why play the fool at all? And why not just inform Louise that you aren't in the market for a bride? If I had really been as naive and foolish as I pretended, I might have believed you to be showing genuine interest, and then you would have had two women to detach instead of one!"

How much was it safe to share? Brenna was not at all the woman he'd assumed, but Rom wasn't about to endanger his mission by making still more assumptions and telling her exactly why he couldn't risk alienating Louise completely.

"Look, you might as well just tell me," she insisted. "If you don't, I will find out from Quinn, or I'll get a message to Lizbet and demand the truth. She's already hinted that Louise may not be quite trustworthy, but I think she refused to say more because she didn't want to dash my hopes of reconciliation. Are you here to investigate her?"

Rom groaned. Who *was* this woman? And how did she manage to make him feel like such a fool? Well, that part was mostly his own fault. First he'd acted like an idiot in front of her, then he'd insulted her, and finally permitted her to draw a knife on him because he'd completely underestimated her. And now she was uncovering all of his secrets without half trying.

But could he trust her? That was a question he had no way of answering, not without speaking to Quinn.

"Why would I be investigating anyone?" he said cryptically. "I live here. I had nothing to do with Louise Seagrave until I moved into Lorenhall, and I never asked for her to flirt with me."

"Lord Griffin," Brenna said, crossing her arms and sounding very much like a parent with a recalcitrant child, "I have been with Lady Norelle for enough years to recognize her training when I hear it. 'Lie if you must, but stick to the truth whenever possible.' If we are on the same side, let us admit it and move forward. I believe we can agree that the faster we conclude this matter, the better for everyone. While I prefer tending bar at The Bad Apple to my life at Evenburg, I am not fool enough to believe I can stay."

Exactly how deep was she in with Lizbet Norelle? Choosing to listen to an instinct that had rarely failed him in the past twenty years, Rom decided to trust her at least enough to warn her.

"Lady Seagrave," he said softly, "you may think me lacking in courtesy and I wouldn't blame you considering my actions towards you to this point. But I would be unable to call myself a gentleman if I didn't consider that we *are* discussing your mother. It must be hard enough to endure her putdowns and complaints, without also having to suspect her of murder. Perhaps it would be better if you allowed Quinn and I to conclude this matter without your assistance."

Brenna stepped forward until only an arm's length separated them. "Louise is *not* my mother," she hissed. "She may have given birth to me, but Lady Norelle is more my mother than she is. A mother fights for her children. Defends her children. Reminds them that they are perfect and important in her eyes, whether or not anyone else can see what she sees. I came here with questions about my family, but I no longer care about the answers. If Louise is guilty of something, there is nothing you can do to stop me from making sure she faces justice."

Rom looked down and could just barely make out the grim set of her lips and the fury in her eyes. With more respect than he would have thought possible only a few hours before, he inclined his head.

"Then I will speak with Quinn. If he confirms your story, I will return to consult with you about the best way to continue."

His response surprised her. Her lips parted and her eyes widened, and Rom was reminded, even in near dark, that she was actually a very beautiful woman. She was also the only woman who had ever held him at knife point, which, he was startled to discover, somehow made her even more attractive.

But she was also rather annoyed, and she still had the knife, so he wasn't about to tell her so.

There was one other line of inquiry that seemed worth risking. "While we are on the subject, have you considered who else might want to kill you? I suppose we ought to make a complete list of the possibilities before determining guilt."

"I'm not sure whether I ought to feel insulted or flattered that you think there's a list," Brenna answered, but she sounded amused. "Truthfully, I don't know how to answer. The most obvious candidates would be Stockton or Eland Seagrave, but my father has been missing for too long to be a very convincing suspect, and Eland doesn't seem either decisive or bloodthirsty enough to resort to murder, especially considering that he has nothing to gain but revenge."

"Anyone from your former life?" Rom pressed.

"My 'former life'?" Brenna mimicked. "By which you mean my sordid years of wallowing amongst the lower classes whilst I worked for a living?"

"I never said that," Rom replied patiently, "and it's hardly fair to lump me in with the others of my class while railing against the exact same sort of prejudice. The nobility are not all vain, idle and rich, any more than the poor are all vulgar and uneducated."

She looked startled, and then rueful. "You're right," she said. "I apologize. That was poorly done of me. And in any case, the answer is no. At least, not that I'm aware of. I won't claim that I didn't make enemies, or that there weren't people who disliked me, but none that I can imagine going to the very expensive trouble of attempting to hire Quinn. Not that I've ever asked after his rates, but I don't imagine his services would come cheaply, should he ever consider hiring them out."

Rom chuckled. "I'm sure he would be gratified by your assessment."

"And I'm just as sure that he'd never admit it."

They both fell silent for a moment, and the only sounds were the voices and laughter from inside the pub.

"I should be getting back," Brenna said finally, "and you should be getting on with your investigating, or whatever else it is you're pretending not to do."

"True enough," Rom said with a sigh. "I would tell you to be careful, but I suspect you would stab me. I also suspect it is the patrons of The Bad Apple who ought to be careful."

A dimple appeared on Lady Seagrave's cheek and she curtseyed. "As compliments go, I've heard worse."

Rom chuckled without much humor. "Let me guess. You've been complimented on your title and your money, and received more proposals per hour than most of us draw breaths."

"I can see you've spent at least a little time at court," Brenna acknowledged wryly. "Is it as bad for men?"

"We certainly receive some share of the pressure to marry, but largely from the hopeful parents of unmarried daughters. You, I would guess, are more of a rarity."

"I can't be the first unattached woman to inherit a title," she grumbled.

"Maybe not the first, but it doesn't happen often. Not to

mention that you have no parents to be approached in the usual way. Interested parties are free to approach you personally, which is a burden most young women don't have to deal with."

"That part isn't the burden," Brenna insisted. "Young women *should* have the freedom to accept or reject their own proposals. What I object to is the men who believe that I am helpless and naive—men who have no idea who I am or what I want, and make no effort to find out because they don't care. They are convinced I ought to tie myself to them out of gratitude for their willingness to make my decisions for me, without ever bothering to ask whether I like making decisions for myself."

Rom grinned at the thought of Brenna Seagrave set loose amongst the dandified posers at court. He almost wished he'd been there to see it.

"There's no rule that says a countess has to marry," he reminded her, "so you can go on rejecting them as long as you like."

"Believe me," she muttered, "I've been grateful for that too many times to count."

Rom knew they needed to leave the alley. The longer they stayed, the greater the chance that they would be seen or overheard, and Brenna had a job to return to. The trouble was, he was enjoying the conversation and didn't want to leave it.

"Do you need anything?" he asked, hoping for a reason to prolong the moment. "Do you have a place to stay and adequate funds?"

"Well now, as to funds, that's why I'm working, love," she drawled, swishing her skirts and sashaying backwards towards the mouth of the alley. "And I've found a place to stay. It's safe, and no one's going to throw me out for my questionable choice of occupation."

Rom grinned. He'd like to see someone try. "I'm sure you know this, but as a part of my duty to Lady Norelle I'm going to caution you anyway. Be wary. Whoever hired Quinn—Louise or not—isn't going to give up, and they probably won't resort to the same method twice."

"Noted." Brenna nodded briskly and retreated still farther. "Though perhaps I should say the same to you. If Louise is upset enough by your rejection to kill me to get me out of the way, she may be upset enough to retaliate against you as well."

"Why would she bother?" Rom shrugged. "I'm too great a fool to be a risk to her, and if she hurts me, she loses her only present chance to form a marriage alliance."

"Unless she already knows she's lost that chance," Brenna pointed out, and rightly so. "By my estimation, she didn't have much money to begin with. She couldn't have afforded that place outright, and has to have thrown near every penny into fixing up the house and restoring its grounds. I'm assuming she did so in hopes of convincing you or some other impecunious nobleman to marry her, so if she's gambled and lost, she might be too sunk in despair to behave rationally."

She was wrong about the money, and the house, but Rom

wasn't in a position to share everything he knew about Louise Seagrave's sordid past. "I'll be careful," he promised instead.

Brenna chuckled suddenly. "I'm sure Danward will warn you if he gets wind of any dastardly plans."

Rom's shoulders slumped in defeat. "Clearly, I need to invest in new henchmen," he proclaimed in disgust. "I can't believe you found him out so quickly."

"Oh it wasn't me," Brenna said cheerfully. "It was my maid who found him out, but I think she might consider him rather dashing, so there's little risk she'll expose him."

"Thank heaven for that."

Brenna turned away and stepped back into the street with one last look over her shoulder. "Oh, and Lord Griffin? Don't take too long to find Quinn, or I might decide that being a barmaid is vastly preferable to being a countess."

And then she was gone, leaving Rom with the uncomfortable suspicion that he'd been bested, and that when all was said and done, he'd rather liked it.

CHAPTER 8

*D*ear Sir,

I find your continued lack of communication unacceptable. Your failure is as egregious as it is disappointing, and if this is what passes for proficiency amongst your associates, I despair of your profession. Clearly your skills have been exaggerated and I will be forced to conclude this matter without your involvement. I expect the immediate return of the full amount already paid, or I will have no choice but to ensure that the outcome of our contract becomes known amongst your potential future clients.

- Grim Hill

A handful of nights later, Brenna decided to go for a walk after dinner. She'd come to enjoy spending her off hours in companionable conversation with whichever of her housemates happened to be at home, but on this occasion she was feeling too restless to sit.

She changed out of her working clothes into a more sensible outfit, reassured Dora that she would be quite safe, and headed off to become better acquainted with Camber.

At least, that was her excuse. In reality, she was filled with nervous energy and desperate for news. She'd heard from neither Rom nor Quinn, and the silence was infuriating. Did they expect her to sit by idly while they solved everything and presented her with a culprit after the fact? And how could she rest not knowing whether Faline was well? Her maid could take care of herself, but she was alone, and there was no telling what she believed about her mistress's fate.

Brenna needed to know what was happening. It seemed impossible to rest or even know how to behave when she had no idea whether her life was still in danger and no way to find out. At that moment, her irritation with the present situation was great enough that she rather hoped the danger was real. She even hoped whoever had tried to kill her would hire another assassin, because the opportunity to cross blades—or merely fists—with someone would make her feel a great deal better. Most of all, though, she just wanted information, and she wasn't going to get it by staying meekly and properly at home.

Brenna took a meandering route down the uneven, cobbled

streets, not particularly bothered by the darkness, at least until she realized she was being followed. When the sound of the same ill-sprung carriage continued to assault her ears, stopping when she stopped and only moving on when she did, Brenna headed towards the wealthier side of town. It was better lit, and the streets there were smoother, so she took her time strolling through the well-kept neighborhoods, watching the other pedestrians. While she waited for her pursuer to make up his or her mind to act, she pondered what she ought to do next.

She could always walk back to Lorenhall and threaten Lord Griffin with a knife again, but as fun as that would be, she needed to be at work the next day and sixteen miles was a long way to go on foot. She could also tempt fate and return to Crestwood with a harrowing tale of escape from some dastardly kidnapper. However, without knowing what Quinn and Lord Griffin planned to do, that hardly seemed sensible, and Brenna was nothing if not sensible. At least most of the time. In Brenna's experience, it simply wasn't possible to exercise prudence in every circumstance.

For example, a prudent woman with a price on her head would stay quietly in the house whenever she wasn't at work, and would definitely not be wandering the streets when she knew someone was following her. She would never learn much of anything for herself—rather she would stay safe, do her job and wait for the danger to be over. But hiding from danger wasn't who Brenna was, even if that was who the rest of the world wanted her to be.

And that, she realized, was very much at the heart of the entire mess she now found herself embroiled in. She had come here hoping to find out who she was meant to be. Was she really Louise Seagrave's daughter? Or was Lady Seagrave a role she was playing —a role that she felt entirely inadequate to fill?

She was happier at that moment than she had been in months. Alone on the dark streets of an unfamiliar city, contemplating the possible motives behind her own attempted murder, waiting to find out who was now pursuing her, she felt alive and free. Fully herself. Did that mean she had no hope of ever becoming the countess she needed to be—the countess who stayed tamely at home, seeing to her estate, appearing at court, and behaving with placid decorum as she married and produced a suitable heir to the earldom?

Or was there any reason to believe that she could somehow do both, as Lizbet had? Would anyone accept her as she was, if she decided to simply be herself?

She was still contemplating the question when a hackney drew up beside her.

Camber wasn't big enough to have many vehicles for hire, but there were a few. They largely plied their trade between these streets and the merchant's district, catering to wealthy women who couldn't keep a carriage but didn't care to walk in order to do their shopping. These vehicles did not, in general, spend much time in Brenna's neighborhood. They also did not follow poorly dressed women walking alone.

The driver called down to Brenna in a thick northern accent.

"Late to be out, my lady. Might you care for a ride to save your feet? Can take you anywhere in town for a silver coin."

Brenna thought about it for a moment and suppressed a chuckle. From where she stood, she could see three couples, two well-dressed men and a small family, all of them clearly enjoying the advantages of more wealth than she could currently boast. If she were a driver, she would have picked any of the other potential fares.

Unless, of course, she were not a driver, but a bit of hired muscle with a contract on a missing heiress...

Brenna grinned evilly to herself, tossed a silver coin to the driver and opened the coach door. "Can't thank you enough, my man. I'm bound for The Bad Apple."

"Thank you, madam." The driver tucked the coin away and tipped his cap as Brenna entered the hackney and shut the door behind her.

The horse began to move and Brenna parted the grimy curtains to watch as the wealthy part of town fell away. It was quickly evident that they weren't headed to any area of Camber she'd visited before. The buildings passing by the window grew close and dark, the streets narrow and rutted. Soon, the cobbles ran out and there was only dirt beneath the hackney's wheels.

Did the driver really expect that she wouldn't notice where he was taking her? Brenna sighed and settled back into the seat. It really was difficult to hire good evil henchmen these days. Unless of course this was Quinn's way of trying to contact her, but she really hoped he would be more inventive.

Surprisingly, the edge of town rolled by and the hackney kept traveling into the dark, where there was nothing but moonlight to reveal the shadows of trees falling across the road. Brenna supposed she ought to stop their journey soon. She really hadn't intended to go for quite such a long walk, but she was still just a little too curious to see where he was taking her.

Fortunately, only a moment or two passed before the hackney finally rolled to a stop. Brenna listened, wondering whether her fate was to be "runaway hackney" or "held up by highwayman." Or perhaps simply "stabbed and left in the woods to die." She would prefer either of the latter, as the former would make it necessary to actually stop the runaway horse, and while that was possible, it involved more athletic exertion than she was properly attired for at the moment.

The door opened, and the driver stood outside, with a heavy scarf tied over his face. "I'm sorry, miss, but this is as far as we go. You'll have to come out now."

Not the runaway horse then.

"What? Why are we not at The Bad Apple? Where have you brought me?" Brenna allowed a bit of hysteria to sneak into her tone, though it was closer to hysterical laughter than tears. "Why are we... we're in the woods! Are we lost?" She stepped into the road and pretended to stumble just as the driver reached out to fasten both meaty hands around her throat.

So that was his game. Brenna lifted one arm over her head and brought the point of her elbow down directly onto her would-be murderer's arm. He yelped as his arm folded, and Brenna stepped in to bring her knee directly to bear on that portion of the male anatomy most guaranteed to bring an offender to tears.

His hands left her throat after that, allowing Brenna to circle behind him and press her boot knife into the side of his neck, drawing both a trickle of blood and a terrified whimper.

"Don't kill me, lady. Please, not the knife."

"Stop sniveling," Brenna demanded. "It's terribly undignified. And why shouldn't I? You were going to kill me and leave my body for the wolves. What do you have for me that might make it worth my while to preserve your miserable life?"

"Nothing!" the man shrieked as her knife pressed deeper. "No, wait, I mean… I was hired! I don't care what happens to you, but I was paid to make sure your body was never found."

"Who hired you?"

"I don't know," he whimpered. "I don't know. It's always by letter. I do odd jobs, now and again. Sometimes for a man named Grim Hill. He wrote to me last night. Gave me a description of you and said where you lived, where you worked. Offered gold if I could take care of you quick like."

Grim Hill. Well that wasn't theatrical at all. It didn't sound like something Louise would do, but then, it wasn't like she knew the woman well. And how had this Grim Hill known where to find her?

"And that's your best story?" she asked skeptically. "You're going to stake your life on something that ridiculous?"

"It's the truth!" the man cried. "I swear it. On my mother, my sister, my grandmother and my wife."

"Don't tell me a weasel like you is actually married," Brenna scoffed. "You're obviously a liar."

"No! I am! I mean, I'm not. I'm not a liar. I have two children! Please don't kill me!" The man broke down into sobs and Brenna let him go, shoving him away from her and leaving him lying on the dirt of the road.

Ugh. If her mother really had hired him, she had terrible taste in henchmen.

Brenna unhitched the horse, cut away the trailing bits of harness and shortened the reins to an appropriate length before using the hackney's step to mount the animal bareback. "Well, I'll be off then. You may report to your employer that I am insulted by the attempts to kill me thus far, and look forward to improvement in the future."

She pressed her heels to the horse's sides. "And yes, I really am going to leave you here," she called back over her shoulder as her mount trotted off into the night.

It was hardly a comfortable ride, with the bits of harness chafing in unmentionable places, but it was better than walking, at least with the distance she had to go. Fortunately, it was a pleasant night, dimly lit by the moon, and not cool enough to cause a chill.

The outskirts of the city appeared quickly enough, and Brenna began to wonder what she ought to do with the horse. Had he really belonged to the man who accosted her, or had the amateur assassin stolen it from a real hackney driver?

She was passing the first few houses when another horse bolted out of a cross street and slid to a stop directly in her path.

"Oh, seriously," she groaned. "Again? Isn't one ill-advised attempt to kill me enough for the evening?"

"Who tried to kill you?"

That angry bass rumble could only belong to one man, and Brenna scowled at him in the dark.

"You are positively the worst rescuer of all time, Lord Griffin. How is it that you never seem to show up until *after* the assassin has had his chance?"

"Possibly because I've never known anyone quite so difficult to keep track of as you," he responded, sounding irritated as he swung down from the saddle. "Also, your charming housemates really don't trust men. They wouldn't give me the slightest clue where to look for you."

"And no wonder, considering that I never told you where I live. How did you find out?"

"Myra." Rom shrugged.

Well that was worth knowing. If Myra was in the habit of handing out Brenna's location to every man who asked, she could have been responsible for telling Grim Hill where Brenna lived. Then again, Grim Hill had to have found out where she was working first, which meant that even if Myra *had* betrayed her, she wasn't the only one.

Brenna decided to take comfort in the fact that her house-mates, at least, had clearly proven themselves trustworthy.

"I can't imagine it would have helped much even if they *had* told you where to find me," Brenna said wryly. "It isn't like I set out on a walk tonight with an elaborate plan to be abducted by a hackney driver and driven out of town. Why are you trying to keep track of me?"

"Why do you think?" Rom strode over to where Brenna still sat her horse, reaching out to grasp the rein as he glared up at her. "I'm beginning to believe Lady Norelle either has no idea what you're like or has an evil sense of humor."

"Definitely the latter."

"That would explain why she didn't warn me how difficult of a task she'd actually assigned. How does a countess end up with so many enemies? And how in the name of Andar did you end up riding a cart horse out of the woods?"

"Why, Lord Griffin," Brenna said with a grin, "I do believe you're even worse at swearing than you are at rescuing."

"Believe me," he retorted, "I am far better at swearing when there are no ladies present. Now, do you need help getting off that horse?"

Brenna decided to award him a point for asking. He hadn't commanded, or simply dragged her off. She'd not expected that much courtesy or respect, judging by his imperious manner on their last meeting.

"Thank you, Lord Griffin, but if I get off now, I'm afraid I'll never get back up and it's still a ways to walk."

"Never fear, Lady Seagrave," he said with a slight hint of sarcasm. "I'm not so helpless that I can't lift you back up if the need arises."

She snorted indelicately. "Lord Griffin, perhaps it has not occurred to you, but I am hardly one of those willowy maidens who can be flung into a saddle with little more than a thought. I'm afraid you wouldn't be able to make good on that boast, so I'll stay where I am, thank you."

To her surprise, Lord Griffin grinned and his teeth flashed in the moonlight. "You underestimate me, my lady."

"Are you bragging or flirting?" Brenna inquired, with far more aplomb than she was feeling. It had definitely sounded like flirting, but why would Lord Griffin be flirting with her? He knew her for what she was—a common orphan playing countess without much success. Was he the sort of man who flirted with all females, or was he no different than the other nobles who were after her lands and her money?

"Neither." The insufferable man stepped back and folded his arms, smile vanished. "I came looking for you to let you know that Quinn has confirmed you have the trust of Lady Norelle. He has also informed me that he's had another letter from the person who hired him to kill you, threatening to expose his failure if he doesn't return what he was paid."

"Did he say who it was from?"

"Someone who calls himself Grim Hill."

Brenna huffed and rested her hands on her mount's withers. "Then he or she has already hired someone else, though their first hire was quite definitively superior. The hackney driver I mentioned previously apparently works for this Grim Hill on occasion, and had orders to make sure my body was never found."

Lord Griffin took a step nearer and his gaze seemed to rake her from head to toe. "And where is this hackney driver now?"

She shrugged. "Somewhere on the forest road, with a much healthier respect for seemingly helpless women than he had when he woke up this morning."

"And you are, presumably, unharmed?"

"He was singularly incompetent."

Brenna was surprised again when Lord Griffin chuckled and patted her horse's shoulder.

"That would seem to indicate Grim Hill knows you poorly enough to underestimate you, as I did."

"If you're trying to impress me, Lord Griffin, consider your attempts a success." It was no less than the truth. He was handsome enough, and she couldn't help but appreciate his broad-shouldered frame, but it was his respect for her abilities that proved unexpectedly appealing. "Do you and Quinn have any further plans?"

A scowl spread across her would-be rescuer's face. "I'm afraid he's been insisting that we should use you as bait."

Brenna grinned. That definitely sounded like Quinn, and, coming from him, was actually quite a lovely compliment. Could *he* have been the one to inform Grim Hill of her whereabouts?

If so, she knew far better than to even suggest such a possibility to Lord Griffin. While he had apparently developed at least some degree of confidence in her skills, she could tell he disliked the idea of exposing her to danger. "You disagree, Lord Griffin?"

"I can hear you getting ready to be angry with me for doubting you," he growled, "so before you say anything, know that my reluctance has nothing to do with your competence and everything to do with my own skin. Lady Norelle would flay me if I allowed you to be battered, bruised, or gods forbid poisoned because we couldn't come up with any better way to catch this Grim Hill."

"Never fear," Brenna reassured him. "Lady Norelle knows perfectly well that I accept full responsibility for my own safety. It's why I prefer to work alone. The only reason I haven't simply dealt with this on my own is the possible involvement of Louise."

"And if it turns out that Grim Hill *is* Louise?" Lord Griffin asked quietly.

Brenna gazed down at him, hoping to somehow convey the depth of her conviction. "Then I will do whatever is necessary to ensure that she returns to Evenleigh to face the Crown's justice. I know my duty as well as you do, Lord Griffin."

"And if your duty is to trust me in this?"

She considered him silently. Did she trust this near stranger with a case so close to her? Could she step back and believe that he would handle the situation with both justice and discretion?

"I don't know," she admitted. "But I'll think about it."

"That's all I ask," Lord Griffin responded with a nod. "Now, Lady Seagrave, would you permit me to escort you home?"

Brenna snorted. "If you insist, Lord Griffin. I'm afraid I'll have to find my noble steed's home first, but then, yes, I would be pleased to accept your company up until the point someone might see us together and ask awkward questions."

"Embarrassed to be seen with me, my lady?" he asked, with a touch of mockery.

"Embarrassed to be seen with any escort," she returned calmly, hoping he would understand it was nothing personal. "Tavern maids don't go about town with bodyguards, you know."

"Sweethearts, perhaps?"

Laughter burst out in spite of her. "Not in our present guises, Lord Griffin. No one would believe you to be honorable about your intentions towards a woman like me, and I can't afford any other interpretation of our relationship."

His voice went low and dangerous. "What is that supposed to mean? And what, exactly, is 'a woman like you'?"

"There's no need to be offended, either on my behalf or your own," Brenna said. "You know perfectly well that if we're seen together, gossip will insist that I'm your mistress, and my life will become a great deal more difficult. And it has nothing to do with you personally. No one is going to assume that any landed lord has an interest in doing the right thing by a tavern maid, even if she happened to be young and innocent and beautiful. You lot marry your own kind."

"You're not exactly an ugly old hag," Lord Griffin growled, drawing another burst of laughter from Brenna. "And what do you mean 'my lot'? That's 'our lot,' or were you forgetting?"

Brenna sighed. "I've tried, Lord Griffin. I've tried very hard to forget. But Lizbet won't let me abdicate, and my brother is busy being an ambassador, so there's no chance I'll be allowed to walk away anytime soon."

Her mount began to shift its feet restlessly, so Lord Griffin took hold of its bridle before looking up at her oddly. "Do you really wish yourself free of your title?"

"Most days, yes," Brenna admitted quietly. She had no idea why she felt moved to confide in a man she barely knew, but some impulse encouraged her to tell him the truth. "I had a good life before all of this happened to me—I was useful, and I loved my job. I always thought I was angry at my father for casting me off, but, as it turns out, he did me a favor. Being Lady Seagrave…" She looked down at him, admiring his stern-jawed silhouette in the moon-light. "I don't know who she is, but I don't think I like her very much."

"How is she any different than Brenna?"

"Brenna," she retorted, "is who you see now. Can you imagine this at court?"

"Actually," he acknowledged with a grin, "I have an excellent imagination, and I can. I think it would be the best thing to happen to the Andari court since Prince Ramsey was named the heir."

"Then you are more optimistic than I have the luxury of being," Brenna responded tartly. "Now are you going to escort me home or not?"

"After you, my lady." Lord Griffin let go of her horse, swept her a bow and gathered up his own mount's reins.

Brenna rolled her eyes in the dark and tapped her mount with her heels. Lord Griffin was not what she'd expected, and while she generally preferred the unexpected, she wasn't sure she wanted it to take the form of a man.

She might end up liking him, and that, she assured herself, would never do. Becoming attached to a handsome, intelligent, dangerous man was just a way of getting her heart broken. She couldn't imagine someone like Rom ever caring for her in return, except perhaps for the same reasons as her other pathetic suitors. And even if, by some miracle, he did like her for something other than her title and her money, she preferred to work alone. Live alone. To be responsible for herself and answer to no one.

Didn't she?

CHAPTER 9

*M*r. Hill,

Our contract is cancelled. The objective is no longer of interest to me, and I have other places to be. Your fees will, of course, not be returned, as I have expended more than sufficient energy in pursuit of your target. As to your assertion that I will have difficulty finding work, the idea is laughable. No one cares about your over-inflated opinion.

If the target is still of importance to you, she is in Camber, calling herself Renee. She's working as a barmaid at *The Bad Apple*, and living on Mill Street in a house with a green door. If you want her dead that badly, hunt her down yourself. Should you have any reason to consider contacting me again, save yourself the aggravation and don't bother. You won't be able to find me.

- Sir

~

Rom strolled down the darkened streets of Camber, leading his horse and wondering what had happened to him. He felt as though he'd been hit over the head with a blunt object.

No, that wasn't it. He felt energized. Fully alive. Angry. Completely content. All of them at once.

And he felt nothing at all like himself. He didn't normally engage in lengthy conversations with young women. They seldom shared any of his interests, as he led a strange life for a nobleman. One that was difficult to explain without lying, which he preferred not to do unless lives were at stake.

But Brenna... she already knew. He didn't have any idea how she knew, but he also didn't know how she'd managed to foil an assassination attempt and still sound bored.

Rom had wondered for years why he never felt any particular partiality for any of the eligible women he'd met, and this was a devil of a time to figure it out. After chasing Brenna around Camber, attempting to rescue her and discovering she was more than capable of rescuing herself, he'd come to an inescapable conclusion—he found competence to be quite devastatingly attractive.

He glanced up to where she rode next to him, relaxed and serene in the dim light. A slight frown creased her features, but she appeared completely at ease with the situation—the dark, her unconventional mount, a murder attempt, and an unexpected escort.

She didn't even twitch when a trio of men stepped out of an alley to block their way, the golden light of street lamps glinting off the blades in their hands.

"Oh dear me," she proclaimed, pressing a hand to her chest. "Methinks they intend to rob us." She cocked her head to one side. "Well, rob you, anyway. I don't look like the sort of person with much to steal."

Rom chuckled. "They'd be disappointed either way. It isn't like I carry a fat purse when I chase distressed damsels into the seedier side of town."

"Tell me," Brenna asked conversationally, "which Lord Griffin are you today? I only ask because a lady ought to always consider the feelings of others. Are you the Lord Griffin who is lamentably confused by the task of choosing his own waistcoats, or the Lord Griffin who might enjoy a good brawl?"

"Why, my lady," Rom drawled, "are you offering to share?"

"What can I say? I'm feeling magnanimous. If you promise to make it interesting, I might even agree to let you have all of them." She batted her lashes at him, and then winked.

And that was that. At thirty-six years old, Rom discovered that for the first and probably only time in his life, he was in love.

It was sudden, he knew. And probably premature. And she would laugh at him if he declared himself. But Brenna—no matter whether she called herself Breanne, Renee, or something completely different—was the woman he wanted. All he had to do was make sure she stayed alive long enough for him to convince her that she ought to marry him.

Wait. Marry him?

The three cutpurses moved in, even as he worried over that thought. Could he actually propose to a woman and expect her to share the life he led? He'd always thought that would be unfair, but if anyone would be up to the challenge, it was Brenna.

The first man struck at him with his knife and Rom simply moved out of the way. The fellow was slow, and his grip was all wrong.

But she was a countess. She had her own life, with many responsibilities. Even if they married, they might not see much of each other, except for the rare moments when he was at court.

The other two men came at him together, and Rom ducked under one's jab, grabbed his arm, and pulled him into his companion's path. They really ought to coordinate their attacks more efficiently.

Perhaps she could travel with him on occasion. It would only improve his cover, if he could pretend to be married, and she clearly wouldn't mind the danger.

Well, not pretend. They would actually be married. If he could convince her.

The first man dove in, making an attempt to tackle him. Rom shoved him to the side, tripping his two companions who immediately scrambled up, cursing. All attempts at subtlety ceased, and the three came at him as one, fists and knives at the ready.

Perhaps he really ought to focus. A well-timed kick disarmed the first thug, and a simple twist of the wrist brought the second to his knees and left his knife in the dirt. Rom punched the third in the jaw hard enough to knock him out, while kicking their blades out of reach. After the second man staggered to his feet clutching his injured wrist, the first one risked going for Rom's throat, and received a blow to the kidney for his trouble.

That seemed to be sufficient to convince them to seek another target. Brenna clapped appreciatively as the two men who were still conscious limped off into the shadows, muttering comments about Rom's mother as they went.

"I think you could have done that faster, but I'll give you extra points for style," she said. "Also, that kick you used to disarm was a bit weak. If you'd broken his wrist, he wouldn't have come back for another round. Are you favoring your left knee?"

If Rom hadn't been quite certain of his affection before, he was now. "My thanks for your instructive commentary, my lady. Fortunately I know better than to expect thanks for saving your life."

"Careful, Lord Griffin," she said with a smile, "or I might get the idea that you've been paying attention."

"Perish the thought," he muttered. "Yes, I injured my knee some months ago in an ill-advised leap off a roof. In my defense, the smuggler I was chasing turned out to be smuggling more than just un-taxed silk. Half his hold was filled with…" he paused. "Sub-stances I really shouldn't be talking about with a countess."

Brenna sighed. "An unidentified powder that explodes when exposed to fire?"

Rom stared.

"I told you, you really ought to trust me."

"I was told that you had the confidence of Lady Norelle, not that you knew all of her darkest secrets!"

"Did you ever stop to think that of the two of us, I might not be the one whose trustworthiness is most in question?"

With that she urged her horse forward, and left him standing in the street staring after her, with the beginnings of a smile growing on his lips.

They left the horse at a convenient livery, where Rom paid for a few days' worth of stabling in hopes that the owner, if it was not the attempted assassin, would come looking for it sooner or later.

Afterwards, he walked Brenna back to a dark corner near the house where she'd found a temporary haven.

"You trust these women?" he asked, guessing what she would say, but needing to emphasize that she ought to exercise caution, even at home.

"As much as I trust you," Brenna pointed out. "I've spent more time with them, and none of them have accused me of being a fool."

"But are you certain none of them would sell you out?" he insisted. "It took no more than a smile and a coin to convince Myra to tell me where you'd gone. It would be far simpler for someone who shares your house to hurt you, and all too easy for this Grim Hill to offer them adequate incentive."

Brenna turned to face him. "Why, because they're poor and desperate?"

"Because they're human," he replied patiently. "None of us are immune to the lure of easy advancement. We all want simple solutions to thorny problems, like how we're going to achieve happiness in spite of all the obstacles life throws in our way. The size of the obstacle isn't the point."

"They're not going to betray me for money, Lord Griffin." She sounded disgusted by the thought. "These women have left their homes, left behind the dream of easy security in exchange for the difficulty of independence. They've left forced betrothals, cruel fathers, thieving brothers, and a whole world that tells them they can't make it on their own. They want to make something for themselves, to choose their own future, and that's more important to them than ease and simplicity."

"You envy them," Rom said quietly.

"I *am* them," Brenna corrected fiercely. "Except I didn't have the courage to make the same choices—that life found *me*. And even then I had people to tell me I was smart, and strong, and worthwhile. They have only each other, and they've been told all their lives that they are weak and foolish and need someone to make their decisions and tell them who they are. But they escaped, and they believe the world can look differently if they don't give up. I have faith in them, whether you do or not."

"Then I will choose to trust them as well," he agreed, clearly surprising her again.

She stopped and folded her arms. "And will you trust me enough to let me be the bait to capture our target?"

"I don't know," he said, looking down at her with a smile. "But I promise to at least think about it."

When Rom returned to Lorenhall, Quinn was making himself completely at home in the study.

"Please tell me you've been doing something more productive than disappearing mysteriously," Rom growled, restraining himself from telling the man to stop sitting on his desk. Quinn only did it to be annoying, because annoyed people made mistakes. Rom didn't think Quinn was testing him exactly, it was just a difficult habit to break.

As expected, Quinn didn't bother to confirm or deny, only responded with a question of his own.

"Did you speak to Brenna?"

"Only after she'd resolved one attempt to murder her, and just in time to disband a potential second. Though that was likely to be nothing more complicated than robbery."

"Has her mother been in contact?"

Rom's eyebrows shot up. "And how would that work exactly? Her mother doesn't know where she is."

"If she's the one who hired me, she has for several days."

Rom had a choice between weary resignation and murderous rage. One of them would probably get him killed, so he slumped into his chair and regarded the sometime assassin with hard, unforgiving eyes.

"You told her. I thought we agreed that Brenna was not to be used as bait."

"Then you didn't listen. I never agreed."

"What information did you divulge, Quinn?"

The sandy-haired man gave back stare for stare. "Where Brenna lives, what name she's using and where she works." He shrugged. "Up to Grim Hill what happens now."

"If you care for Brenna at all, why would you endanger her?"

Quinn's expression was cold. "What gave you the impression that I care for anyone? Whoever hired me needs to be caught. I took the most straightforward path."

"And if the most straightforward path leads to Brenna's death?" Rom snarled.

Quinn jumped off the desk and strolled for the door. "She's more than you give her credit for, Lord Griffin." He glanced back.

"And it might interest your man at Crestwood to know that I conveyed that information by letter."

Rom's eyebrows shot up. "Since when do real assassins send letters?"

"Since they needed one to be found. As evidence."

Sneaky bastard. It still didn't give them good odds. If Louise was Grim Hill, she had been devious enough to avoid getting caught, at least up to this point. It was unlikely she would keep the letter, unless she was hoping to use it. If she was angry enough at the man who had accepted a contract to kill her daughter and kept the money despite his failure, she might keep the letter as proof. And if she did, Danward might just be able to discover it.

But if they were wrong, and Grim Hill was someone else...

"You'd better hope Danward finds something."

"Or what?" Quinn replied, his voice filled with quiet menace.

"Or I might not care that we're on the same side and you'd probably kill me. If anything happens to Brenna because of this, I'll come after you."

Quinn shrugged. "Love makes fools of the best of us." He stepped through the doorway, looking back over his shoulder long enough to add: "But you could definitely do worse."

The door closed just in time to catch the paperweight Rom hurled viciously in Quinn's direction.

The following evening, Brenna returned home from work to find all seven of her housemates waiting for her in the sitting room, wearing identical expressions of uneasiness and strain.

Brenna was already nursing a sore ankle, numerous abrasions from her unexpected ride, and an overwhelming sense of discontent. She couldn't identify it exactly, but she suspected it had something to do with a certain irritating nobleman. A tall, strong, competent, intelligent nobleman who looked at her with admiration instead of disdain.

Lord Rommel Griffin ought to be ashamed of himself for invading her thoughts so comprehensively.

"Is something wrong?" she asked, hoping that whatever it was could be resolved quickly and with minimal involvement on her part.

"This." Grita pointed to a basket that rested on the small, round table in the center of the room. "Did you know about this, then?"

"It's not mine, so no," Brenna said, confusion mingling with impatience. "What is it, and why would I know about it?"

"It was left here for you," Dora informed her, with uncharacteristic seriousness. "An old woman brought it and asked to see you. When I told her you weren't here, she left it for you, and said we weren't to open it without you. That our very lives might depend on it."

Brenna's heart dropped. "You didn't open it, did you?"

"And why should we not have?" Grita demanded. "Unless you have something to hide?"

"We were suspicious," Batrice explained, rather mildly. "And curious. It just seemed odd. What could someone be leaving you that was so important and that only you were supposed to see?"

Brenna looked around the room, counted again, and noted that all seven women appeared to be unharmed. Perhaps it wasn't what she feared.

"We all have things to hide," she reminded Grita firmly. "And we promised not to dig into one another's secrets. I don't mind if you opened it, but it would be safer for you to leave my problems to me in the future."

"With secrets like this one, we might not all *have* a future!" Grita snapped. "You owe us an explanation!"

Brenna sighed and moved closer to the table. "What happened?"

"We heard something moving," Batrice said quietly, "so we decided we'd better find out what it was."

She picked up the basket, turned it over, and dumped it out. A pile of laces and ribbons slithered out onto the tabletop, along with the dark, sinuous body of a very long, very poisonous, very dead snake.

A krait.

"Well, that's certainly not a very nice present," Brenna said into the ensuing silence. The other women just stared in horrified fascination. Brenna leaned over the table and observed that the snake's head had been separated very cleanly from its body. "Who killed it?"

Sinna raised her hand. "Grew up on a farm," she said with a shrug. "Had to know how to kill things."

Brenna nodded. "And the woman who left it?"

"Old," Dora said. "At least, she wanted me to think so. She wore a hood, and she sounded old. But her hands were smooth."

Brenna shuddered a little as she imagined sweet, gentle Dora carrying the deadly basket into the house. The venomous creature could so easily have been set loose amongst women who had no idea of its true destructive potential.

Had it been her mother, this old woman with young hands? Was Louise capable of such hatred, such disregard for life? If she was, Brenna needed to be gone from here. She could not continue to endanger other lives merely to protect her own.

"I'm sorry," she said, meeting the eyes of each woman in turn. "Sorry that you were caught up in this. I had no idea that my troubles would follow me here. I'll be gone as soon as I can gather my things."

"Oh, no you don't." Grita's arms were folded and her eyes narrowed to slits. "Even if you leave, this person could be back, and you owe us the truth."

Brenna met her eyes coolly. "Are you sure you want it? Makes no difference to me, but once you have it, you can't go back."

"Try me," Grita said challengingly.

The other women looked back and forth, from Grita to Brenna.

"Fine." Brenna put her hands on her hips. "My real name is

Lady Breanne Seagrave, Countess of Hennsley, and I'm hiding in Camber under an assumed name because I was the target of a professional assassin who may or may not have been hired by my mother."

Dora gasped, and Batrice's eyes grew avid and bright.

"I think," Grita said dryly, "that you'd best start at the beginning."

So Brenna did.

A few nights later, The Bad Apple was bursting at the seams with enthusiastic customers. It was payday for most of the working men, and they were happy to share their wealth with Myra, who was quite willing to receive it in exchange for beer, bread, and stew. Brenna was familiar with most of the regulars by that time, and stopped to converse with several as she passed with her hands full of mugs, dirty dishes, trays and towels.

It was loud, wild, and jovial, and she loved it. Sadly, it would probably all be over soon. Rom had sent word that he'd instructed Danward to search for a letter, written by Quinn to the mysterious Grim Hill, revealing Brenna's whereabouts. If it could be found in her mother's possession, their mission would be complete.

Rom had been furious at what he was convinced was Quinn's betrayal, but Brenna thought it a stroke of genius. This sort of ruse would never work on a seasoned criminal mastermind, but was more than worth the attempt in this case. They needed to sort this out quickly, and Louise was likely to be desperate. In Brenna's experience, desperation bred mistakes.

The krait, for instance—and its method of delivery—had most assuredly been a mistake. If Dora was correct, Louise might have actually brought the basket herself, risking discovery and even death had the creature escaped. The risk of collateral damage had likewise been enormous, and still gave Brenna nightmares. Probably would have given Rom nightmares as well, if she'd had the nerve to tell him about it.

The train of her thoughts brought Brenna up short as she realized that she'd stopped thinking of Louise as merely the most likely suspect. At what point had she begun to believe without question that her mother wanted her dead? Also, when had she started thinking of Lord Griffin as simply Rom?

Brenna's arms were both loaded down with trays when the noise and bustle of the tavern suddenly ceased. Every head turned to the door, every breath caught in a motionless throat. Brenna turned too, carefully, so as not to spill, unsure what it might take to silence the entire room. She should have known.

Louise Seagrave stood in the doorway, clothed in glittering, jewel-encrusted satin, with emeralds around her neck. Her golden hair was piled high upon her head, and her hands were gloved in silk. She looked as though she'd just prepared for a ball at Evenburg rather than an evening out in a pub. She also looked absurdly young for a woman of almost fifty.

When Brenna said nothing, only raised a curious eyebrow, Louise lifted a gloved hand beseechingly.

"I have found you at last, my darling. You don't know how worried I've been these past days, wondering what might have happened to you. But you're here, and you're safe, and now you can come home with me and everything will be all right again."

She sounded as though she were auditioning for a part in a play.

Brenna blinked and set her trays down. "I beg your pardon?"

"Brenna, please, you know that I love you. Can you not forgive me for wanting only to care for you as a mother should?"

It took tremendous effort not to roll her eyes. "How did you find me?"

"Rom told me he'd seen you, and that you've been calling yourself Renee, of all things. He was terribly worried about you, my dear." Louise took a tiny step forward, her hands clasped in supplication. "I know you begged him to keep your secret, but I have told him so many times of how much I dote on you, how much I was looking forward to helping you fill your new role as Countess of Hennsley, so he told me everything. I hope you're not angry."

As certain as she'd felt of her suspicions before, ice entered Brenna's heart as they were finally confirmed. Rom would never have told Louise anything. The only way for her to have known that name or where to find Brenna was through Quinn's letter. Beyond all question or doubt, Louise was Grim Hill.

It was enough for Brenna, but it wouldn't be enough for

Crown justice. They were going to need real, physical proof if they hoped to convince anyone else.

Brenna opened her mouth to respond but she was interrupted by one of her customers, who stood up so abruptly that his beer sloshed over his hand to splash onto the floor.

"Just hold on there!" The man set down the mug and wiped his hand on his shirt. "You're a bleeding countess?"

"No, I'm afraid I'm just a countess," Brenna said wearily. "But that doesn't make me incapable of serving beer."

"Well, I don't want your ruddy noble hands touching mine," another man sneered, provoking a chorus of laughter. "Who knows but what some of those fancy manners might be catching!"

The man whose arm she had threatened to break on her first night stood up, his lips twisted in dislike. "Who do you think you are, anyway? Pretending like you're a barmaid when you're really some bleeding noble. Like it's some kind of joke? Were you having a laugh at our expense, then?"

"I'm just working, Petey," Brenna snapped. "Same as you. I work for a wage and I pay my way. What she calls me makes no difference."

"But... Brenna, darling, of course it makes a difference," Louise objected in shocked accents. "You're different. You're something special. You shouldn't be here with these rough types, picking up coarse habits and vulgar language. You should be at home, with me, where I can mold you into a countess all of Andar can be proud of."

Suddenly, Brenna realized what her mother was doing, and silently applauded the tactic, even as she cringed at the effect Louise's words were having on the crowd. Sentiment was rapidly turning. Where most of the crowd had been willing to laugh at first, more and more heads were turning to look at Brenna with hostility.

Even Myra walked out from behind the bar with a tense, angry stride. "And just how many lies did you tell me, hoping to sweet talk me into giving you a job? Making me feel sorry for you." She crossed her arms and her eyes sparked with outrage. "I shoulda known better when that Lord Griffin came round asking for you. You said you'd got no place to live, but it sounds to me like you've got a mighty fine one, and a mother who seems to think you're a mighty fine pet. Why don't you go on back and play dress up and leave us rough folk to our coarse habits and vulgar language." Myra leaned forward deliberately and spat on the floor, before turning her back and walking away.

The crowd stood almost as one, and their expressions were anything but friendly. Brenna shook her head in disbelief, but there was nothing she could do. Louise had done what she'd come for. She'd poisoned the entire crowd against Brenna and made it impossible for her to stay.

How had it taken so little for them to turn against her? For the past two weeks she'd served them, laughed with them, learned about their families and proven she knew how to work hard, just as they did. She had more in common with them than she did with

Louise, and yet the moment they heard her title, it was not enough.

"Very well." Brenna took off her apron, folded it neatly and set it on the table next to her trays. "I'm sorry," she said into the overwhelming silence. "Sorry for wanting to make my own way and be something other than useless and decorative. Sorry for not wanting to be like her." She waved disdainfully at her mother's glittering form. "I never meant any harm, and I don't believe I hurt anyone by choosing to work for my living instead of having everything handed to me. I'm just sorry you can't accept that—or accept me in spite of my birth."

The first one took her by surprise. As a full mug's worth of beer caught her in the face, Brenna gasped, and barely managed to duck the second, which was flung at her head mug and all. A bowl of stew was next, and struck her in the arm before cascading down her skirt in a greasy waterfall of meat, potato bits and broth.

After that, the barrage intensified, as the outraged patrons vented their feelings with flying food and the occasional piece of flatware.

Brenna abandoned her dignity and ran for it. She had enough presence of mind to notice that her mother had disappeared, but was too preoccupied with saving herself to spare much thought for where that much satin could have disappeared to without a trace.

She was almost to the door when something heavy struck her on the temple and the whole world went black.

CHAPTER 10

$\mathcal{L}$ord Griffin,

I've enclosed the incriminating letter, as you requested. Further search confirmed a possible interest in poisons, so be wary. If it eases Lady Seagrave's mind, you may tell her that I've long since taken the liberty of informing her maid of the situation, though Miss Faline seemed both unsurprised to learn of her mistress's survival and entirely unconcerned about her safety in the future. I swear I've done nothing to indicate the truth of our presence here, but she also made it clear to me some days ago that she was aware of my duplicity and has apparently harbored suspicions regarding my honesty since shortly after entering the house. In fact, it was Faline who aided me in gaining access to Louise Seagrave's private papers, and the success of this endeavor might be said to have depended entirely on her cleverness and ingenuity.

I've never asked this before, as there has never been reason to consider it, but have you a firm policy on courtship and marriage amongst your retainers?

- Danward

~

He was always just a moment too late. Rom took in the suddenly silent scene with a murderous glare as he bent over Brenna's still form. She was almost entirely covered in gravy, drenched in beer, and a knot was forming on the side of her head.

Rom was just brushing her hair back to get a better look when her eyes fluttered open and blinked at him.

"You're late, as usual," she murmured. "You really need to work harder at this rescuing business."

He chuckled in spite of his anger. "How about if I carry you home to prove that I can manage at least one thing properly?"

"As I've told you before, Lord Griffin, you can't carry me anywhere. I'm no willowy maiden, to be swooning about expecting a man to sweep her up in his arms."

Rom grinned and winked. "Maybe I shouldn't," he said, "but never tell me I can't."

Without waiting for further protest, he picked her up and turned to face the surprised crowd. "You lot ought to be ashamed.

If you have a grievance, you talk it out like men. You don't attack a woman like a pack of wolves."

"She had no business bein' here," one of them muttered. "Lied to us, she did. Let us think she was one of us, when all the time she's got a fancy house and a fancy title."

"Then would you like to throw some soup at me?" Rom snarled. "Or am I exempt because I buy you beer and act like you've decided a nobleman should?"

"You never pretended to be anyone but who you are," Myra said with a glint in her brown eyes. "She led us to believe she was poor and alone. That she needed us. We helped her and this is the thanks we get—her hoity-toity mother coming in here to talk down to us?"

"So," Rom returned coldly, "you attacked a woman, for no better reason than not liking the family she was born in? Would you want to be judged by your parents? Weighed and measured by what people expect from looking at your past? How would you feel if this was another pub somewhere, and this woman was your sister, or your daughter?"

He didn't give them a chance to answer, just stalked out the door and into the dark street. "My horse is nearby," he said. "It won't be a comfortable ride, but I can get you back to Lorenhall and find someone to see to your injuries."

"The first thing you're going to do is put me down," Brenna demanded. "It was a nice thought, and I appreciate you proving that you're fully as strong as you look, but I believe I can walk."

"If you're sure." Rom lowered her feet to the ground, but didn't let go of her shoulders just yet. She staggered a little as she tried to stand, but gained her balance after a few moments.

"Thank you," she said, her hand still on his arm. "I appreciate it. I think they were fully prepared to drown me in beer if you hadn't come."

"What happened?"

"As Myra mentioned, it was Louise." Brenna's voice sounded pained. "I think she was hoping to deprive me of a job so I'd have to go back to Crestwood and be murdered in peace. She told them a countess was serving their drinks and they rioted."

"When was she here?"

"Just now. You didn't see her?"

Rom shook his head. "She was nowhere in sight when I walked up."

Brenna's face grew grim and cold. "Rom, it was no accident that she found me. She knew exactly where to look and what name I was using. She's definitely the one, I just don't know how to prove it."

Rom placed his hand over hers, his heart hurting for her discovery. He couldn't help a surge of satisfaction when he realized she'd used his name, but this wasn't the time to tease her about it.

"Don't worry," he reassured her. "We can prove it now. My man Danward worked together with your maid and found the letter in Louise's study." He felt her whole body sag just a little before she caught herself and stood firmly upright.

"I feel like there's a story there," Brenna said dryly. "It wasn't that long ago Faline was complaining of Danward's highly unbutler-ish behavior. However did he convince her to trust him?"

"If Danward's letter can be believed, she considerably more than trusts him," Rom admitted. "And he sounds utterly besotted with her."

"Oh dear." Brenna took off her scarf, wrung it out, then retied it to keep her hair out of her face. "Definitely a story. But we can't go back until we find Louise. She's already proven she's willing to hurt others to get to me."

"Is there something you haven't told me?" Rom couldn't think of anyone Louise had injured other than Brenna herself.

"She put a krait in a basket and sent it to my house," Brenna answered curtly.

A chill spread through his body and he flexed his fingers against a swell of anger. "Even I wouldn't have dreamed she'd go that far, but—"

Brenna interrupted suddenly, her eyes gone wide.

"Rom, that means she knows where my house is!"

They looked at each other and broke into a run.

Rom let Brenna set the pace and kept an eye on her to ensure she was sufficiently recovered, but she seemed none the worse for her adventures as they dashed across two streets and headed for the tiny house with the green door. Despite the inhabitants' dislike of men, Rom didn't pause at the gate, or even the walk, but raced after Brenna up to the door and through it, all the way into a tiny sitting room where they burst into the middle of a very strange scene indeed.

Louise Seagrave held court at one end of the room, her satin skirts spread about her ankles, her hands folded demurely in her lap. Brenna's seven housemates were collected at the opposite end, regarding the former countess much as they might have regarded a roach, or a rat in the larder.

"Ah, Brenna, my love, there you are..." Louise stopped and her eyes widened just a trifle. "Rom? Whatever are you doing here?" Her gaze darted around the room. "Is there no rule against gentlemen callers?"

"Aye, but there's also a rule against prating harridans, and we've already broken that one," a tall, grim-looking brunette ground out. "Now say your piece so we can kick your arse back onto the street again."

"I am only here for my daughter," Louise said, her dignity slightly marred by a welling of tears. "All I want is to take her home. I have gone on for too long believing her dead, or worse, and I could not bear to leave her here in wretchedness and squalor when she should be with me." She wiped her eyes with a lacy, white handkerchief that promptly disappeared again back into her sleeves, or wherever else ladies kept such objects. "I had to rescue her," she went on, glancing up at Rom beseechingly. "Did you come to help me?"

A grimace spread across Brenna's face. "Rescue me, Mother? You caused a riot at The Bad Apple and then left me to their tender mercies. If you wanted to rescue me, that would have been the appropriate time."

"I only wanted you to see how uneducated and vulgar and base such men could be," Louise insisted. "I never dreamed they would actually hurt you."

"Well, they did, and you didn't stay to find out, did you?" Brenna pointed out. "You abandoned me to my fate and came here so you could intercept me when I ran home in tears. You hoped after all your efforts I would fall neatly into your loving arms and trot off home where you could have me at your mercy once more."

"I..." Louise looked shocked. "Of course I want you to come home! Brenna, my love, there is so much left to do. So much more for you to learn." She turned to Rom. "Please, you must help me convince her, Rom. You know I can be of help to her, and how ruinous it would be for her to stay here. You've seen how much she needs me! I cannot allow her to be further corrupted by the manners and morals of the lower classes, which, under the present circumstances"— she cast a glance at the seven women across the room—"would be inevitable."

"Yes, Rom," Brenna said sweetly, "do help her convince me to go home. After all, Mother says it was you who told her where to find me. Apparently you were so concerned for my welfare that you went to her and told her everything."

Rom turned a cool stare on his neighbor. "Really, Louise? And how can it be that I don't remember telling you any such thing?

How did we have an entire conversation that then somehow completely slipped my mind?"

Louise lifted her eyebrows and shrugged delicately, appearing unconcerned but for the clenching of her hands in the silken folds of her skirts. "I haven't the smallest idea how you could have forgotten. You came to me last evening and told me you'd seen her here when you visited the pub. Perhaps the strain of the past days has been too much for you and your memory has grown hazy, but I remember." She smiled up at him with warmth and feeling. "I don't know that I can ever thank you enough for your efforts on behalf of my poor daughter. Without you, I might never have known she was so close, and that I still had a chance to take her home and love her as a mother should."

"Enough," Rom growled, barely suppressing a shudder. How Brenna could have such a poisonous creature for a mother would never cease to amaze him, and he was done playing the fool for the sake of her vanity. It was time for her to know that the game was over and she'd lost.

"I know you think me a buffoon, Louise, but that's because I wanted you to think it. I have forgotten nothing. The very last thing I would have told you is the whereabouts of your daughter."

The former Lady Seagrave merely looked perplexed. "I don't understand, Rom. We're friends, you and I. We've discussed my hopes and dreams for Brenna many times. Why would you claim now that you would hide her from me?"

"Because I know exactly who told you where to find her," he

said, letting Louise hear every bit of the vast well of his contempt. "It was Quinn. The man you paid to assassinate your daughter because you couldn't live with the knowledge that you're not the countess anymore."

Louise froze, and her eyes darted from Rom to Brenna, and back again. "I don't understand," she said at last, confusion beginning to give way to cool withdrawal. "Who could even invent such a story? It's positively barbaric, to imagine that I would hurt my own child. Why would you insinuate such a thing?"

"It's not insinuation, Louise," Rom said coldly. "It's the truth. We finally have all the proof we need to accuse you of attempting to murder the Countess of Hennsley, and it's only a matter of time before we find proof of the rest."

"The rest?" Brenna said, turning on him sharply.

Louise burst out laughing. "You can't possibly have proof of something I haven't done," she said. "And no matter what lies you choose to tell, who is going to take your word over mine?"

Rom met her eyes and let his lip curl in disdain. "You mean, who is going to believe the word of a great, lumbering ox of a man who cannot tell when he's being played for a fool by a conniving harpy in pursuit of a title?"

Her face grew pale and her eyes glittered dangerously, while her hands shifted in the folds of her dress. It seemed she had at last begun to perceive that the conversation was not going quite the way she'd hoped.

Brenna interrupted. "Rom, what did you mean by 'the rest'?"

He didn't take his eyes off Louise as he answered. "As you suspected, I was sent here by the Crown to investigate certain suspicious coincidences that seemed to occur all too often in association with Louise Seagrave. Lady Norelle believed she was never the silent, unwilling partner in Stockton's schemes. When we discovered that she purchased Crestwood in secret over five years ago, using funds that mysteriously vanished from the estate's accounts, it set us on the trail of other, not-quite-legal activities. Like tax avoidance, transportation of illicit substances, forgery... I could give you quite a list."

"You can prove nothing," Louise said, a smile tugging at the corner of her mouth. "And buying a house is not a crime. Protecting myself from my husband's numerous ill-advised ventures and embarrassing infidelities might, in fact, be called prudent."

"Yes, it might," he agreed. "If you'd stopped there. But you were the one who arranged for your firstborn child to be switched so that you would have a male heir. It was you who convinced Stockton to hide the truth, you who encouraged him to disappear rather than suffer the consequences of your actions, and you who ensured that he disappeared permanently from a ship to Thalassa last year."

Brenna took a step back and looked at Louise, her eyes narrowed. "Is it true?"

The woman held herself with fragile dignity as she faced them, still seated but uncowed. "I would never hurt my child," she said softly. "Whatever I have done, I can only beg you to believe that I have done out of a mother's love. I want only what is best for my heir, and right now, the best is for you to come home where I can give you the future you deserve. If you stay here, among the lower classes, your vulgarity will only be encouraged and you will never gain acceptance at court. Is that what you want?"

She turned to their audience, who were watching with expressions of mingled horror and fascination. "If you call yourselves her friends, is that what you would want for her?"

Rom winced. Louise was apparently looking for a repeat of what happened at The Bad Apple, but the seven women only regarded her with folded arms and stony glares.

"And I thought *my* mum was harsh," one of them said with a derisive snort.

"The best place for your daughter is wherever she wants to be," the grumpy-looking brunette said. "We're not kicking her out on your command. When she's ready to leave, that's fine, but you've no right to tell us who lives in our house."

"But I'm trying to save her," Louise insisted. "Someone has already tried to kill her once, and it could happen again."

"So we should send her back to you, where she almost died the first time?" the brunette said sarcastically. "Seems to me, she's been safer here than with you, unless you know something we don't." There was a challenge in her voice and a glint in her eye, but Louise wisely decided not to take the bait.

"You must know that her presence here could be putting you

all in danger," she insisted instead, leaning forward in her chair with a pleading expression. "If Brenna goes with me, everyone will be safer."

"Everyone except me," Brenna retorted, hands on her hips. "Louise, we know it was you who hired Quinn to kill me. We have proof. His letter was found. You can keep prating forever about how much you care for me, but no one will believe you. It's over."

Louise rose to her feet at last and regarded them all as though she were a queen, not a disgraced former countess. All pretense of solicitude seemed to fall away from her face, to be replaced by a mocking sneer.

"You?" she said incredulously. "I, care for *you?*" Her laugh was razor sharp and pointed. "I have never spared a moment's affection for the pitiful *thing* my husband planned to pass off as our heir. *You* are nothing but living proof of Stockton's feebleminded scheming and serial infidelity."

Rom's gaze darted to Brenna, and he saw her eyes go wide as the blood drained from her face. She jerked forward with her hand outstretched, the motion appearing almost involuntary, and Rom reached for her arm just a moment too late.

Louise had finally concluded that her charade was entirely useless. Her hand darted out from the folds of her dress holding a jeweled dagger—not the fake, decorative sort, but a true weapon with a deadly sharp blade. She took two quick steps forward, grasped the front of Brenna's shirt in one tiny fist, and held the razor edge of her weapon to Brenna's throat.

Brenna stopped the instant she felt the cold metal brush against her skin, and met Louise's murderous stare with icy calm, despite gasps and cries of alarm from the women now ranged behind her. "Are you going to stab me with that, Mother? Slice my throat? Or drive it through my heart, as you hired Quinn to do? Are you so obsessed with revenge that you would rather kill me than see me take your place?"

"This has nothing to do with revenge!" Louise hissed, the blade trembling in her hand. "This was never about me! Everything I am, everything I have done, is for the sake of my beloved child. My only child. The title, the lands, the power—all of it should be his!" Her eyes narrowed as she leaned closer. "My Kyril is the rightful Earl of Hennsley and I will never stop, never rest, never be at peace until justice is done and you are exposed as the illegitimate pretender you truly are!"

Brenna's jaw would have dropped, but there was the knife and Louise's hand was already shaking. Any movement would be a bit of a risk.

But even the knife felt unimportant next to Louise's words.

Could she be telling the truth? Kyril... her only child? If so, Brenna's life was about to be turned upside down once again.

If Louise was not her mother, then Brenna was not a countess after all. She might not even be a Seagrave. So many months she'd spent wallowing in self-doubt and insecurity over the Hennsley title, and for what? So she could lose her identity once again? And not only her identity—her home, her source of income, her brother...

Brenna's heart suddenly seemed to be trying to pound its way out of her chest, and she wasn't entirely sure of the reason. Was she afraid of losing the wealth and position she'd spent the better part of a year learning to live with? Afraid of losing Kyril? Or was she desperately hoping to find that she shared no part of Louise's blood, even if it meant she was once again penniless and alone in the world?

The older woman's steely blue eyes left no doubt that she, at least, believed with every fiber of her being that Brenna had no part in her life.

"Is it true?" Brenna whispered.

"I would have known," Louise said, her lip curling in contempt, "if I had given birth to something like you. But if you want proof, I can provide it. I kept the record of your birth because I knew this day might come."

Truth. In spite of all Louise's lies, Brenna's instincts screamed that this, at least, was no deception, and all she could feel was an overwhelming sense of relief.

A tight, hard knot in her chest loosened and she took a breath, feeling lighter than she had in months.

Breanne Seagrave did not exist. Had never existed. Somehow, she was just plain Brenna Haverly again, just as she'd known herself to be for the first twenty-seven years of her life.

She thought she should probably feel something more than just relief. Bereavement, regret, sadness... She should be angry. She should feel betrayed, but all her heart was capable of was emptiness and confusion.

"Then why?" she said softly. "Why did you ask me to come here? How did any of this ever happen? I believed for most of my life that I was the illegitimate daughter of Stockton Seagrave. If that was true, why didn't you say so ages ago and end this charade?"

"I couldn't," Louise said, clearly frustrated by the restriction. "Not without losing my place at court forever. I had to plan everything perfectly so I could be there to see it when my son came into his rightful inheritance. This was the only way."

Brenna opened her mouth, but Louise pressed the knife closer to her neck as her eyes darted to Rom.

"No closer," she hissed. "Or I slit her throat here and now."

"Why haven't you?" Brenna taunted, shifting her feet to give herself the best chance at evading a sudden strike. She could most likely disarm Louise if she chose, but not until she'd gotten the full story. She needed it too much to stop now. "If you're not going to explain yourself, just do it. Kill me here and now. Then Rom will strike you down before you've had a chance to tell anyone the truth. No one will ever know why you did what you did, and Rom will make sure you're remembered as a mother so twisted that she murdered her own daughter out of spite."

Louise laughed and twisted her grip on Brenna's shirtfront. "Oh, my dear, do not make the mistake of assuming that either you or Rom have any power here. I will take your life when I'm ready, and then I won't care what becomes of me. My main goal will be achieved. I did plan to regain a title for myself so I could stand by my son's side as he rises to power, but it is enough to know that the earldom will be his."

Rom interrupted, his voice low and urgent. "It could still be his, without the need for murder. Why not just tell everyone the truth?"

"Because I'm the one who told His Majesty about Brenna in the first place," Louise snapped.

Brenna heard rustling and whispering from behind them, but she ignored it. "That seems a trifle shortsighted," she said, putting as much sarcasm into the comment as she could muster. "Why not tell them then and there that Kyril should be the heir?"

Louise looked as though she'd bitten into something sour. "I faked my first pregnancy," she announced bitterly. "I thought I couldn't have children, so when I found out Stockton's mistress was expecting, we decided to claim the child as our own. At least until we found out it was a girl. Fortunately, the mother died in childbirth, so I convinced Stockton to exchange it for a male child and we went on pretending."

Brenna almost couldn't draw breath as she contemplated the full truth of what Louise had revealed. Brenna's real mother, the woman who'd given birth to her, was dead—had been dead for twenty-eight years—and Louise could only call it "fortunate."

She somehow managed to control her disgust and contempt

long enough to ask another question. "But if you couldn't have children, where does Kyril fit in?"

"When I became pregnant with him," Louise said, her expression softening, "it was a miracle. I wanted to get rid of Eland even then, but Stockton wouldn't let me. He'd grown fond of the brat, despite the fact that he was no blood of ours, though I suspected he could have been one of Stockton's that he'd never bothered to mention. Stockton even threatened to cut off my allowance if I ever gave so much as a hint that I favored Kyril. He was so worried about being found out that he forced me to treat Eland like a prince, and my own flesh and blood like a useless second son."

She'd wanted to get rid of Eland. By this point, Brenna didn't even try to talk herself into believing that Louise meant something other than murder.

"So you just went on as you were, for years," Brenna prompted, "and I was raised as an orphan, though the earl must have told someone the truth because I at least knew he was my father."

"Yes." Louise looked as though the admission pained her. "He told the woman in charge of the home that you were his daughter, gave her extra money to make sure you were well taken care of. I warned him it was too dangerous, but he never listened to me. And then?" She grimaced. "Everything fell apart. The woman who raised you talked to someone who actually listened. About Eland, and about you. Stockton came to me in a panic, and Eland heard us talking. He was furious, and said that he wanted to meet you. To see if it was all true." A smirk crossed her face. "You can believe that I made sure that woman wouldn't be talking to anyone else, but the damage was done, and the only way to salvage the situation was to tell the Crown myself that Eland was a fraud and you were the real heir."

A chill ran down Brenna's spine. That woman had a name. Mrs. Orrin. The woman who raised Brenna until she was twelve. She hadn't had much warmth to spare for her charges, but she'd been the first mother Brenna knew and she'd been murdered to further Louise's twisted ambitions.

"How can you say that was the only way?" Brenna demanded furiously. "There was no need to kill Mrs. Orrin! You could have told the truth and then Kyril would have been the heir just as you wanted!"

"Except that the gossip had already spread too far! Too many people already knew about you and believed you to be legitimate!" Louise grew flushed with anger, and the hand holding the knife faltered. "Eland turned out to be a spineless fool, just like Stockton, and he could never keep a secret. Perhaps I should have gotten rid of him as I'd always planned, but then you would still have been in the way, and two deaths would have looked suspicious."

"So the only reason you didn't murder Eland is because you thought you'd rather murder me?" Brenna couldn't quite comprehend such a cavalier attitude towards death.

"It had nothing to do with preference," Louise insisted, as though Brenna were quite dim for suggesting it. "I had no clear path to disinherit you once the court knew you existed. Better to let them rid me of Eland legally, and then I could deal with you however I wished in my own time."

Brenna heard a low, rumbling chuckle from just behind her shoulder.

"You got a poor bargain if you thought you could deal with Brenna however you wished," Rom pointed out. "I've met Eland, and you'd have had far better luck with him."

Brenna risked turning her head to look up at him and for a moment the emptiness of her heart seemed to ease. "Thank you," she said, the corner of her mouth curving up.

"No more than the truth, my lady," Rom replied with a courtly bow, but Brenna could see that his lightheartedness went no further than the surface. There was fear in his eyes, and anger in the set of his jaw, and she knew she could not expect him to remain a passive observer much longer.

She returned her attention to Louise, realizing that despite her many experiences with the criminal underbelly of Andar, she had never despised anyone quite so completely as she did the woman she'd once believed to be her mother. But there was one question that still needed an answer.

"You still haven't explained why you didn't simply tell the truth," Brenna repeated once more. "If you'd gone to them and admitted that you faked your pregnancy—that I was never your child any more than Eland was—none of this would have needed to happen."

Louise merely shrugged. "Even if they would have believed me, I could not allow them to know that I lied," she said. "Every other deception could be blamed on Stockton. After all, everyone believed me when I claimed that he forced me to say that Eland was my child. That he forced me to remain silent about you. But there was no way to deny my part in faking my own pregnancy and claiming you as our heir. Had I admitted to either of those, my reputation would have been in ruins and all my other plans would have fallen to nothing."

Shocked silence followed that announcement, and even Brenna could find nothing to say. Louise had committed murder to preserve her reputation?

"You've got a lot of nerve calling *us* the lower classes," Sinna interjected scornfully. "You'd have it that *we're* the ones who are going to encourage vulgarity? We might not dine on silver plate and wear satin every night, but at least we'd never dream of doing something so vile as murdering an innocent woman to protect a lie!" She threw up her hands. "You're a monster! And I've no doubt you'd have killed all of us as well, just to get to her!"

"I would have killed anyone who got in my way!" Louise said fiercely. "I knew from the moment Kyril was born that I would do anything for my son. For the first time, I had a child who was the image of me, not Stockton, and whenever I saw his face I knew I would have done far worse than murder for his sake."

This. This was the depth of feeling Brenna had long believed ought to define a mother's relationship to her child, a feeling that had been missing in every one of her encounters with Louise. At least now she knew why. It had nothing to do with her own inadequacies, and it horrified Brenna to see what should have been a beautiful, protective love twisted beyond recognition into a foul and murderous compulsion.

She wished suddenly that she could somehow protect her brother from ever finding out what his mother had done in the name of her love for him. Because no matter what Louise said, no matter who Brenna's real parents were, Kyril would always be her brother.

Louise turned her gaze back to Brenna and her voice broke a little. "Why couldn't you just have died?" she pleaded. "Then everything would have been as it should. Even if Rom hadn't married me, I'm still beautiful enough to attract a man in need of what I can offer. With a title, and a fool like Rom as a husband, I could have smoothed my son's way at court when he took his rightful place. Rom would never have gotten in my way as Stockton did, and then when I didn't need him any longer, I could have kept his title for myself!"

"Tell me," Rom responded dryly. "Was there anyone you *weren't* planning to murder?"

"Clearly she wouldn't have hurt Kyril," Brenna replied, noting that her voice sounded rather more normal than she would have expected, after all the shocks she'd had. The knife at her throat didn't even seem to matter much at the moment. "Which is lucky for her. If she threatened my brother, I think I'd have tried to break her nose, which is probably a worse punishment than death for someone as vain as she is."

"You act as though you're so much better than I!" Louise said disdainfully. "You've done nothing but lie and pretend since the moment you arrived in Camber. You pretended to be a fool to humiliate me, and you pretended to be no better than a common barmaid to worm your way into this house. You don't deserve their loyalty, or anyone else's after the part you've played in this deception."

"Deception?" Grita echoed. "She told us the truth, you stupid old hag. She told us exactly who she was, who sent that wretched reptile, and why. We knew she was a countess and we chose to let her stay. Because she's no different than us. We all know what it's like to have families we'd rather not admit to. Did you really think that just because we're poor and uneducated, we'd stand back and let you kill her?"

Louise's smile sharpened. "I don't see how you can do anything about it now. I have the upper hand here, and even Rom wouldn't dare risk any heroics with my blade at her throat. The lot of you can do nothing but watch whenever I decide to take her life."

Brenna resisted the urge to roll her eyes. Eventually she would have to relieve the woman of that particular delusion, but not yet. Not until this was truly finished. "Well, before you murder me, then, since you've been so kind as to tell me the truth about your actions, I feel it's only fair to tell you the truth in exchange."

Her gaze hardened and she leaned forward, ever closer to the hand that grasped her shirt and the knife that lay coldly against her neck. She saw Louise's eyes widen, but pressed on until she sensed the other woman's weight shift backward in confusion and saw her nostrils flare in alarm. Brenna felt the sting as the skin of her neck parted beneath the edge of the dagger, but in that moment the pain mattered less than the need to throw Louise off-balance. To force her to listen.

"You've gone to all this trouble," Brenna said. "Invited me here, pretended to like me, hired assassins, imported poisonous snakes and revealed your hand in front of a Crown agent... when you could have just asked me."

"Asked you what?"

"Asked me to step down," Brenna said simply. "I would have handed Kyril the earldom without question or argument. Stepped aside gladly, whether my birth was legitimate or not, because I love him far more than I love being a countess." She held Louise's cold blue gaze and let the other woman see the full measure of her scorn. "You could have had it all, Louise, but you threw it away out of misguided hatred. You assumed that everyone else values power as much as you. Fears exposure as much as you. But all I ever wanted was a family—not the title, not the lands, but someone who would love me. Someone to belong to. You saw only what you wanted to see, and it's that blindness that has destroyed all your plans and brought you to the end of this road."

Her blindness, and Brenna's too. If Brenna hadn't been so desperate for someone to tell her who she was, she never would have responded to that invitation and none of this would have happened...

But then again, she couldn't regret all of it. She wouldn't want to have missed meeting Rom, or Grita, or Sinna, or any of the other women she'd so briefly shared a home with. And she didn't regret finally coming face to face with her own prejudices.

Much like Louise, she'd been guilty of judging the world by her experiences. But the nobility as a whole did not deserve her disdain, any more than the working class deserved her wholesale approbation. For every nobleman who had offered her a back-handed proposal, there was a Rom, a Caspar, or a Kyril, who respected and listened to the women in their lives.

And it was no different amongst the members of any other class. She'd been assaulted in hatred by the men at The Bad Apple for no better reason than her title. A complete stranger had been willing to kill her in exchange for money. And yet, the women she shared a house with had chosen to side with her, even after her secrets endangered them.

People were far too complex to be merely one thing or another. A man could be a courtier without being pretentious, and a woman could be a flower-seller with the heart of a lion. Whatever had made Brenna think she had to be either a countess or a spy?

Louise seemed frozen in the wake of Brenna's statement, until Grita finally broke the silence with an ultimatum.

"I have better things to do than listen to more of this. Would one of you decide what's going to happen next so we can all get back to work?"

The hand holding the dagger shook, by now with strain as much as emotion. Louise had been holding it at Brenna's throat for several minutes, and her arm was no doubt growing tired. When the older woman shifted her weight from one foot to the other, Brenna seized the opportunity.

Without a sound she jerked backwards and dropped to the floor. Tilted her head away and fell, letting her weight tear her out of Louise's grasp and carry her out of range of the deadly blade.

Rom let out a hoarse cry. "Watch the knife," she heard him say. "It may be poisoned."

He probably thought her injured, but she rolled away too quickly to be taken for a corpse.

It might still have gone badly had they been facing a woman with experience in physical confrontations. Brenna's skirts were too sodden for her to sweep her adversary's ankles, and they likewise prevented her from regaining her feet as quickly as she preferred. Fortunately, Louise was a creature of drawing rooms and polite fencing matches, and she reacted to Brenna's fall far too slowly to do any good. Brenna was already on the floor before the former countess screamed in frustration and launched herself forward, at exactly the same moment that Batrice threw herself into the midst of the scene. The acrobat flipped across the room, striking Louise's wrist with her heel and sending the jeweled knife spinning across the floor into a corner.

"No!" Louise darted towards the weapon, but Rom moved far more quickly than one would expect from a man of his bulk. He caught her around the waist, lifted her off the floor and deposited her none too gently on a chair.

"Louise Seagrave, you are hereby charged with the murder of Stockton Seagrave, the murder of Mrs. Orrin, and the attempted murder of Breanne Seagrave. In my capacity as an agent of the Crown of Andar, I order you to appear before a royal court and answer to the king's justice."

Louise did not react quite as Brenna would have expected. Her face was pale and set, but she didn't even seem flustered by Rom's announcement. She merely smiled, while her eyes remained fixed on her husband's daughter.

"It's too late," she said softly. "You should have known better than to believe that I could fail in the one great purpose of my life. After twenty-seven years of waiting and planning I have finally succeeded. Before tomorrow dawns, Brenna will be dead, my son will be the earl, and I... I will have won."

CHAPTER 11

*D*ear Lady Norelle,

Please find enclosed my completed report on the Seagrave matter, including what I believe will prove to be sufficient evidence to pursue two of the charges under investigation. There has been some delay as we have sought to define the full extent and nature of the accused's most recent crimes. Given the lack of clarity in both the intent and outcome of her actions, I have chosen to enclose a list of possible future charges for your consideration, which I will be pleased to discuss with you upon my return.

At that time, I will also be pleased to discuss the numerous omissions and roundaboutations which have led to a great deal of unnecessary hazard and misunderstanding on the part of myself and other participants in these recent events. Allow me to express my utmost certainty that should you at any point in the future require an agent to be responsible for the wellbeing of yet *another adventurous countess, you may consider me entirely unwilling to serve.*

The prisoner and her escort are en route, and I encourage any and all possible efforts towards making their stay in Evenleigh as uncomfortable as possible.

- Rommel Griffin

∼

A chorus of gasps surrounded Brenna as she rose shakily to her feet.

"Stop being melodramatic," she said firmly. "I'm not returned from the dead—the blade cut me, but there's barely a scratch."

"Unless she's poisoned you." Sinna, the apothecary's assistant, moved to Brenna's side as the other women gathered around. Batrice went to the corner to retrieve the dagger.

When Brenna pressed her fingers to the stinging line on her neck where the dagger's edge had left its mark on her skin, they came away covered in blood.

Rom looked down at her over Dora's head, his brows drawn together with worry. "How deep is the cut? Do you feel dizzy? Any pain?"

"I feel fine." Brenna shrugged as she eyed the dagger in Batrice's hand. There was definitely something coating the edge of the blade, so she took it and sniffed at it before handing the weapon to Sinna.

The red-haired woman examined the knife, careful to avoid contact with her own skin, and then smelled it as Brenna had done. She also examined Brenna's neck with careful fingers as the rest of the room held its breath.

"You were right," she announced, smiling in a way that indicated vast relief. "It *is* poisoned."

Rom growled harshly and shoved his way to Brenna's side, putting an arm around her shoulders as though he was afraid she might faint. "Then what do we do? Is there an antidote? Can we find a doctor nearby?"

"Probably." Sinna shrugged. "But I don't think she'll be needing one." The grin on her face grew a little.

"I won't accept that!" Rom argued desperately, turning to grab both of Brenna's shoulders in his large hands. He searched her face, his mouth set, eyes a little wild. "There has to be something we can do. I'm not just going to let you die, Brenna, I swear it. If anyone knows where the doctor is, I'll take you there myself! Just tell me how to fix this!"

"Well," Sinna rubbed her chin thoughtfully, "I've heard that some maladies can be cured by a good kiss, but I suppose we wouldn't know unless you tried it."

Rom turned his head to glare at her. "How can you joke about this?"

Brenna burst out laughing and tugged at his sleeve. "Rom, I'm not dying. Sinna, tell him what it is."

"Oh, the poison? It's oleander," Sinna said, her eyes twinkling. "At least I'm fairly sure of it."

Rom's eyes shut and his shoulders slumped as he let out a low growl that probably would have turned to violence had he not been surrounded by women. "I think you just took five years off my life," he muttered, finishing by rubbing one hand through his already rumpled hair. "Do you think His Majesty would let us charge Louise with causing you a violently annoying rash?"

Brenna chuckled at his expression. "Well, she thought she was going to kill me. Surely we could call it something more official sounding. Like 'poisoning without adequate information.'"

"I'll be sure to put that in my official report."

"Then, you're going to be all right?" Dora whispered, her freckles standing out more than usual against her pale skin.

"Most definitely," Brenna assured her. "Louise should have done her research a little more carefully. Oleander is poisonous, but it has to be ingested to be very effective. I suppose if she'd managed to stab me with the blade, it might have hastened my death, but it would have taken considerably more than a scratch."

She turned towards the window, expecting to see her mother either quivering with rage or stunned in defeat, and saw only an empty chair.

Brenna rolled her eyes and sighed. "Rom, where is Louise?"

"Out the door, while you lot were fussing about poison," Grita informed them, her mouth twisted in distaste.

Rom swore and started towards the door, turning back to Brenna just before he got there. "I'm going after her. Will you be all right?"

"What do you mean will I be all right?" Brenna snapped in irritation, wiping her bloodied fingers on her already ruined skirt. "I'm coming with you, you ridiculous oaf."

Their eyes met and held.

"Are you sure?" Rom asked carefully. "She's finished now, and she knows it. She won't go quietly or easily."

"I don't care," Brenna told him fiercely. "She's tried three times now to kill me and I think I've earned a part of this."

Rom nodded and his eyes warmed as he held out a hand. "We'll do this together, then?"

Brenna's breath caught in her chest. Whatever he meant, the look in his eyes suggested it might be more than simple camaraderie. "Yes?" she said, and placed her hand in his without hesitation.

Rom closed his fingers around hers and led Brenna out the door into the darkened street. He didn't let go as they walked first one direction, then the other, searching without much urgency, knowing that wherever Louise had gone, she could no longer escape justice.

In the end they didn't have to look far to find the quarry they sought. Only two streets away, across from The Bad Apple, half in, half out of the thoroughfare, a glittering pile of satin lay crumpled in the dirt. Gems on the skirt sparkled in the light from the open door of the tavern, while a man stood in the shadows nearby, watching as Brenna and Rom approached.

"Quinn," Brenna muttered. "Of course you were sneaking around waiting for us to flush her out. What happened? Did she say anything? What did you do?"

Quinn lifted his head and regarded her impassively. "She tripped," he said blandly.

Brenna regarded him with one raised eyebrow. "Over what? Your foot?"

"You'd rather it had been my blade?" he inquired.

No, she did not wish that. It might have been a mercy, as the Crown would most likely sentence Louise to die, but Brenna thought it more fitting that the former countess should have the chance to face her accusers and endure the agony of a public court proceeding. Let justice do its part. Brenna had no desire to end this chapter of her own life's story in blood and violence.

There had been enough of that already. Her mother. Mrs. Orrin. Her father. Who knew how many more had died to satisfy Louise's desire for power and control?

No doubt the rest of that story would be told, and Brenna's heart ached for her brother, who would have to learn the full, terrible truth about his family. But as for the rest? Brenna would pursue justice for everyone involved, but she no longer felt the need to uncover more about her past.

She had mistakenly believed that if she could know where she'd come from, she could determine who she ought to be. That understanding her past would help her find her way between her duties and her desires. But when she'd learned that her parents were long dead, she'd felt nothing. No grief, no regret. All of her family that mattered would be coming home soon from Caelan. Kyril and Ilani, and shortly thereafter, a new Seagrave, who would be heir to Hennsley—its grounds and its wealth, at least. Brenna desperately hoped the next generation could avoid the Seagrave legacy of deception and violence.

And as for her?

"I'm not a countess anymore," she whispered, more to herself than anyone, but Rom heard her.

"Actually," he said soberly, "you are."

"What do you mean?" Brenna couldn't see how that was possible. "If I'm illegitimate, I can't inherit."

"You can't," he agreed, "but you didn't exactly inherit in the usual way. You were officially named countess by the king. Now, it's no different than a peerage bestowed by right of merit."

Brenna's jaw dropped. "Then I'm still stuck? And Kyril can't be the earl?"

Rom chuckled. "I'm sorry if that disappoints you," he said. "Perhaps you should take some time to think about it. If you consider all the options and end up wishing to abdicate in favor of your brother, I believe His Majesty would understand."

"So you're saying I have a choice?"

"Of course!"

As she watched Quinn crouch down to bind Louise's wrists, Brenna allowed herself to consider Rom's words. Could it really be that easy? Had she always had a choice who she wanted to be, and simply never seen it for what it was?

Maybe it didn't matter what the court expected of her or what they thought a perfect countess ought to look like. Maybe it didn't even matter who her father was or who had raised her. Perhaps all she needed to remember was who she had chosen to be. A woman who loved her family. Who cared about justice. And who had chosen to dedicate her life to protecting her kingdom.

"Can I really just be Brenna?" she asked softly, of no one in particular.

"Of course you can," Rom scoffed from beside her. "Who else would you be?"

Brenna looked up at his rugged features and began to laugh. "It really is that simple, isn't it? I know it sounds like a strange thing to say, but I feel like I haven't been doing a very good job of it lately. And yet you just reminded me that perhaps I shouldn't have been trying so hard in the first place."

"What were you trying to be?"

"A countess," she admitted. "I've been trying so hard to be the perfect countess that I've forgotten how to be Brenna. And I didn't think I could be both, but... maybe I can." She laughed and closed her eyes. "Maybe I can be a countess and an accountant, or a clerk and a spy. Or all of them at once if I want to be."

"Wait—" Rom turned to face her, took her other hand and lifted an eyebrow as he gazed down at her. "I know we've established that you're cozy with Lady Norelle, but...you're one of her spies?"

"What, did you think all countesses learned how to disarm rowdy bar patrons?" she asked archly. "Or how to threaten strong, handsome and overbearing men with a knife to their kidneys?"

"You think I'm handsome?" A grin crept over his features.

"Trust you to focus on the least important part of that sentence," she retorted.

"I just don't understand how I've never met you before. How long have you been with Lady Norelle?"

"How do you know you haven't met me before?" she suggested with a sly wink. "I am *very* good at my job."

"I would have noticed you," Rom insisted. "And can I just say that I'll be having strong words with both the Norelles for keeping me in the dark about all of this. And for making me think you were someone who needed protecting. I've been worrying myself half to death about you, when I should have been worrying about who needed to be protected *from* you!"

"Careful, Lord Griffin," Brenna said sternly. "I'm an impressionable young woman and if you don't moderate your compliments, they may turn my head."

Rom's eyes went bright. "Is that a promise?"

"If the two of you don't mind," Quinn said, with what almost sounded like sarcasm, "we have a prisoner to be taken up and transported."

Rom looked over his shoulder. "Oh, do you need help?" he asked in mock surprise. "I had no idea. You've always seemed so overwhelmingly competent."

Quinn's face could have frozen a white-hot forge.

"I'd be happy to transport the prisoner," Rom went on genially, "as long as you're willing to assist Brenna in searching the house for evidence and compiling the report in preparation for trial."

Quinn regarded them both impassively. "I think I'd prefer to be as far away from the two of you as possible. I'll tell Lady Norelle to expect you in no more than a fortnight. And no getting lost on the way home."

As he shouldered the limp body of Louise Seagrave and disappeared into the shadows, Brenna watched him go and wondered where, exactly, home might be.

She honestly had no idea, but for once, the idea felt bright and beautiful, rich with possibilities.

Home wasn't a place, and it never had been—not Crestwood, not Evenburg, not Norleigh. Perhaps home, for her, had more to do with the people she loved.

No matter what she decided to do about the earldom, she would still have Kyril in her life, and Ilani, and Lizbet, and Faline. And maybe, if she had read him correctly, she might just have Rom. It was a strange new thought, but she welcomed it.

There was still much to be done. They would need evidence of

Louise's other crimes. Kyril and Ilani would be home in a few months, and her brother would be more than a little blindsided by the news of his father's death and his mother's duplicity. There would be a trial, and all of the Seagrave family's embarrassing history would be paraded before the court in humiliating detail.

But Brenna felt strangely free. She finally knew who she was, and it had nothing to do with her name or her heritage. No matter whether she chose to keep her title or not, she was a woman, a sister, a daughter, and a friend. A countess, a clerk, a barmaid, an accountant, or a spy—what she saw in the mirror didn't matter, because she was free to choose whether or not to be content with herself.

And, at long last, she knew that was enough.

In every way that mattered, Brenna Haverly had come home.

No matter how hard she tried, Brenna couldn't seem to stop smiling. She smiled at the guards as she passed through the gates, at the servant who took her cloak, at the debutantes who stared at her escort, and even at Prince Ramsey when he stopped to greet her politely.

"Stop smiling," Rom whispered in her ear. "They're going to think you're up to something."

"Maybe I am," she whispered back.

She smiled even wider at Lizbet, when she caught her mentor's eye across the room, and she had a special grin for a dazzled but undaunted Batrice, who was taking in the scene as Lady Norelle's newest and most enthusiastic protégée. But Brenna smiled the widest of all when King Hollin performed the ceremony that proclaimed a stunned-looking Kyril Seagrave to be the newest Earl of Hennsley.

Ilani stood nearby, looking very pregnant and deeply proud of her husband, though she'd confided privately to Brenna that she was a bit concerned about how they were going to manage their new responsibilities.

"I've found a replacement who will do well enough while I'm absent, but I cannot imagine who will take Kyril's place while we're adjusting," she'd pointed out. "No one else in Andar knows our people as well as he does, and he's actually quite popular in my brother's court."

Of course he was. Kyril somehow managed to be popular everywhere. It had once irritated Brenna beyond all reason, but now she found it amusing, even endearing. It was a gift, the way he managed to be likable to nearly everyone, and it would serve Andar well now that her brother had found his place.

Much as she had. After long consideration and a great deal of discussion with Lizbet and Caspar, Brenna had decided it was best to pass the title on to its rightful owner. Not because she couldn't wait to be free of it, but because it was the right decision. For Kyril, for the kingdom, and for her.

"How long until we can leave?" Rom muttered, as they observed the congratulatory throng surrounding the new earl and countess.

"Where are we going?" Brenna asked, surprised. "I didn't think we were heading out until Danward and Faline get back from their wedding trip."

"We're not," Rom confirmed, turning a slightly odd shade of

red. "Lady Norelle says that our ship won't be ready to sail for a few more weeks at the least."

"Are you that desperate to escape?" Brenna asked, patting his arm. "I know, this isn't my favorite either, but I promised Kyril I'd be here for him, and you have to admit, it's fun to watch Eland turn purple thinking about the future heir to Hennsley."

Considering what she'd learned about Eland's past, Brenna thought she might not have been entirely fair in her judgements of the man who might actually be her half brother. She'd invested considerable time and patience in attempting to make it right, but he hadn't been making it easy. He was still a pompous twit, who'd been stiffly polite up until she'd announced her intention to abdicate in Kyril's favor.

After that, he'd pointedly avoided her, more out of fear for his person, she suspected, than anything else. Brenna wasn't sure whether he'd believed her former threats or was completely intimidated by Lord Griffin's size and grim demeanor, but Eland seemed unwilling to reconcile himself to either her presence or Kyril's inheritance. If he was likewise distressed by the downfall of the woman he had once called Mother, he had not been willing to share those feelings with Brenna.

"I don't care about Eland," Rom grumbled. "And I wasn't talking about our mission. I had something else in mind."

"Like what?" Brenna asked absently, as she hugged Parry Norelle in passing. The boy was already taller than her, and looking very handsome these days. It wouldn't be long before the younger debutantes started taking notice, and then wouldn't Lizbet be grouchy as a bear.

"I know I should have said something before..." Rom began, only to be interrupted by the approach of one of Brenna's former suitors, who bowed over her hand.

"So delighted to see you've returned," the fellow said pompously, pointedly failing to release her hand at the appropriate moment. "I must say, the court has been quite dull without the brilliant light of your beauty to brighten our days. Would you favor me with the pleasure of a dance, later?"

Brenna burst out laughing. At first, she hadn't expected any of her suitors to renew their feigned interest in her, not once it became clear that she'd chosen to give up the title. Sadly, it seemed to have gotten around that the new earl intended to settle a generous inheritance on his half-sister, and an alarming number of her former swains seemed intent on capturing it for themselves.

"Were they always this ridiculous?" Rom snapped, clearly irritated by the interruption.

"Worse," Brenna told him sweetly, removing her hand from the man's grasp, and curtseying politely. "I'm sorry, but I don't really want to dance with you. Have a pleasant evening."

The fellow gaped like a fish and remained stationary, his hand still out, as she steered Rom in the opposite direction.

"And how exactly is it ridiculous for him to call me beautiful?" she asked, eyebrow arched as she glanced up at her friend's scowling face.

"That wasn't the ridiculous part, and you know it," he said. "He wasn't any more delighted to see you than I am to be here."

"And I thought *I* hated court," Brenna said with a laugh. "Poor Rom. It's a good thing the trial has concluded and we're leaving in a few weeks, or you might need to be sedated."

It had taken time for evidence to be gathered, but in the end Louise Seagrave had indeed been found guilty of the murders of Stockton Seagrave and Eileen Orrin. The evidence of Louise's numerous attempts to kill Brenna had scarcely been necessary, and she'd been sentenced to death by an implacable King Hollin.

Brenna had felt nothing, either at the woman's conviction or her execution. Perhaps she would someday, but she doubted it. Even Kyril had scarcely mourned, reminding her that he, too, had suffered through his parents' coldness and cruelty as a child. Brenna had never been more grateful that she and Kyril had somehow found each other and could be reminded daily by their own relationship that they need not go on as their parents had.

"Actually," Rom said, looking at the floor, "I had a rather better idea what we ought to do with the next two weeks."

"Oh, do you have a mission?" Brenna's already buoyant mood brightened still further. She wouldn't mind getting out of the city and keeping her mind occupied until they sailed.

"In a manner of speaking. At least, I'm hoping to." Rom looked around, growled something under his breath, and grabbed Brenna's hand. "I hate crowds," he muttered, heading for the nearest door.

Brenna was quite willing to follow him as he made his way onto a balcony that appeared to be deserted. She didn't much care for crowds herself, and his behavior was growing increasingly strange.

"Rom, what is it?"

"We're leaving in a few weeks," he said, leaning against the balcony rail and avoiding her eyes.

"Yes," she drawled, "I'm quite well aware."

"And we'll be gone for some time. Pretending to be married while we hunt down Frenish spies."

"Is this going to be a problem?" Brenna's brow wrinkled in concern. "We discussed it with Lizbet, and we agreed that it was the best cover for our mission. Have you changed your mind?" Her heart sank a little. She had so been looking forward to this trip—just her and Rom, enjoying a friendship that had become ever more valuable to her since their return from Camber.

He wasn't just a fellow spy—he was the only person besides Lizbet that she'd ever felt truly understood her. Respected her. Even admired her. He'd never tried to take anything away from her accomplishments or her career, and actively sought her opinions.

She would miss that, if he chose not to work with her. She would miss *him*. She'd come to adore his solid, thoughtful presence, his keen ability to anticipate her moves in a fight, and even his grumbling, when life forced him to take a break and simply be himself.

"Are you trying to say you don't want to do this with me?" she asked. Her voice trembled a little, which only made her angry at herself. She didn't want to let him know how much the loss would affect her.

"No!" His response could not have been more forceful. "That's not what I'm trying to say at all. I was about to suggest that maybe it would be easier if we... that is, perhaps we ought to..." His chin dropped to his chest and he rubbed the back of his neck. "I wondered if you might rather not pretend."

"I suppose we can come up with a different cover story, if you prefer," Brenna said hesitantly, trying to conceal her hurt.

"No, I mean... Egad, I'm ruining this, aren't I?"

Rom reached out and took her hands in his. "I'm really just trying to ask you to marry me before we leave. I know it's a bit scandalous not to have a long betrothal, but I really don't want to pretend to be your husband. I want to be yours for real."

For a moment, Brenna couldn't breathe.

He'd just proposed. Rom had proposed. She'd wished and she'd hoped, and she'd had ever so many proposals before but never one that made her feel like her world had turned inside out and presented her with everything she'd ever wished for.

"You really... you really want to marry me?" she whispered.

"Only since the moment you put a knife to my back and said 'never tell me I can't.'"

Brenna laughed until she felt tears run down her face. "Why didn't you say anything before now?"

"Because," Rom said, reaching up to brush tentative fingers

across her cheek, "I don't have anything to offer you. All I have is an empty title. There's a little money, but no home, no future. I didn't think any woman would ever want to share that with me. But you?" He dropped to one knee—which put his head only slightly lower than hers—and looked into her eyes with unmistakable certainty. "No matter how much nothing I have, I will always want to share it with you. No matter how hard things get, they're infinitely better if you're there. I didn't mean to ask this soon, but when I realized we would be pretending to be married, I just couldn't help it." He chuckled. "If you were willing to sail across the ocean and pretend to be stuck with me, I thought maybe you'd be willing to be stuck with me for real."

"Rom, I've wanted to be stuck with you for ages."

"You'll have a title again," he reminded her. "You'll have to endure being called Lady Griffin and making occasional appearances at court."

"I've made my peace with that," she pointed out, "and besides, it also means that no one will ever propose to me again, which more than makes up for any potential aggravation."

"At least they'd better not," Rom growled, rising to his feet and pulling her tightly to his chest. "Because I'll…" he stopped.

"You'll what?" Brenna asked, smiling up at him.

"Never mind me," he said, grinning suddenly. "If they're smart, they'd be more worried about what *you* would do to them."

"That's right, and don't you forget it," she said, or at least she meant to say it, but was interrupted somewhere in the middle by

Rom's kiss. It was fierce, yet tender, and when he lifted his head again Brenna was sure the whole world had shifted and would never be the same.

"Wait, did you ever actually say yes?" he asked curiously.

"More or less," she assured him.

"I'd prefer a more. Just in case your brother decides to take offense at my suit."

"Kyril?" she scoffed. "He's my *younger* brother. He doesn't get to take offense. And besides, if he decides to be difficult, I'll threaten to tell Ilani how he got his reputation as the most scandalous flirt ever to grace the Andari court. And also, yes."

Rom picked her up and twirled her around, happier than she'd seen him in ages. "Are you going to want to go back in there and dance now?"

"I'm sure we can think of something better to do to celebrate our engagement," she demurred. "Like chasing down smugglers, or capturing a murderer or two."

"And I thought I loved you before," Rom said softly, looking down at her with glittering eyes.

"Want to go jump off a roof?" she asked with a smile.

"Anything," he answered. "As long as it's with you."

THE END

◞◟

THANK YOU

Thank you for reading! I have loved writing this series and getting to know its characters and I hope you have enjoyed going on this journey with them. For more of their adventures, check out the rest of the series, or sign up for my newsletter to be the first to find out about new releases.

http://kenleydavidson.com

If you loved Daughter of Lies and want to share it with other readers, please consider leaving an honest review on Amazon or Goodreads.

Not only do I love getting to hear how my stories are impacting readers, but reviews are one of the best ways for you to help other book lovers discover the stories you enjoy. Taking even a moment to share a few words about your favorite books makes a huge difference to indie authors like me!

OTHER BOOKS

THE ANDARI CHRONICLES

The Andari Chronicles is a series of interconnected fairy tale retellings
that evoke the glittering romance of the originals, while infusing them
with grit, humor, and a cast of captivating new characters. *If you enjoyed
the world of Andar, be sure to check out the other books in the series:*

Recommended Reading Order:

- *Traitor's Masque*
- *Goldheart*
- *Pirouette*
- *Shadow and Thorn*
- *Daughter of Lies*

http://kenleydavidson.com/books

ABOUT THE AUTHOR

Kenley Davidson is an incurable introvert who took up writing to make space for all the untold stories in her head.

She loves rain, roller-coasters, coffee and happy endings, and is somewhat addicted to researching random facts and reading the dictionary (which she promises is way more fun than it sounds). A majority of her time is spent being mom to two kids and two dogs while inventing reasons not to do laundry (most of which seem to involve books).

Kenley is the author of The Andari Chronicles, an interconnected series of fairy tale retellings, and Conclave Worlds, a romantic science fiction series.

She also writes sweet contemporary romance under the pseudonym Kacey Linden.

kenleydavidson.com
kenley@kenleydavidson.com

ACKNOWLEDGMENTS

When I wrote Shadow and Thorn last year, I planned for it to be the last of the Andari Chronicles for a while. I was happy with where the story ended, and felt comfortable leaving that world to its own devices until I had written a few more books. But, as they often do, a few characters kept nagging me for their own stories.

Brenna was one of them, so after three books in other worlds, I couldn't help returning to write her a happily ever after of her own. As is usual when my stories begin, I had not yet met all of the characters. Even Louise was no more than a shadowy shape in the background of Brenna's life, so I was very much surprised to learn what she'd been up to for all those years and what sort of man Brenna was going to fall in love with.

I suppose the lesson here is that I should never underestimate the power of a strong character to find their own story. There will no doubt be more in the coming year—Blaise is growing impatient, Parry Norelle is growing up, and it won't be forever before Rowan finds a way out of his prison. But for now, I hope you have enjoyed getting another glimpse of Andar before I'm off again to sail through rifts in space and meet more of the quirky inhabitants of Echo Creek.

I have a few new people to thank this time around, but I can't even begin to talk about this book without crediting my usual team of co-conspirators...

- Janie, my editor, whose hyphenation super-powers never cease to amaze me (should super-powers even have a hyphen?)

- Tiffany, who read it twice in order to reassure me that it really wasn't as terrible as I thought it was.

- And Jeff, who didn't even roll his eyes once when I told him exactly what kind of model I needed for the cover design.

In addition to my always-supportive beta team of Mary, Chloe, Larry, and Chandra, I am also deeply and permanently indebted to the ladies of The Indie Bunch, my amazing crew of author friends who have joined together to encourage each other on our authorial adventures. K. M. Shea, Brittany Fichter, Shari L. Tapscott, Aya Ling and Melanie Cellier—you ladies are an inspiration and a joy to share this journey with. Since meeting you all, I have laughed far more than I've cried at the crazy ups and downs of writing.

My gratitude also goes out to Lanie, who found so many incredible ways to make this story better and encouraged me not to give up even when it seemed like the book was never going to come together. I am so looking forward to writing alongside you in the future.

To Melanie—your last minute read through was incredibly helpful and I am so thankful for the gift of your time and expertise.

And finally to my readers, as always, I am deeply grateful. You continue to make it possible for me to do what I love, which is a gift that cannot be overvalued. I am thankful every day for your reviews, your tweets, your messages, and your emails—they remind me that my stories are not simply words on a page, but a way of connecting with people I would never otherwise have a chance to meet.

Thank you!

Made in the USA
Monee, IL
15 January 2021